Published by Under the Moon, LLC
Pelican Rapids, MN

Take Down
ISBN: 978-1-938339-27-1
Copyright © 2015 Terri Pray
Cover Art Copyright @ 2015 Samuel Pray and Terri Pray
Editor in Chief: Terri Pray
All rights reserved.

Take Down

Author's Note

Fiction is a wonderful distraction, but in real life D/s and BDSM should be entered into with knowledge and trust. If you have an interest in the lifestyle or even occasional play, please follow the rules of either Safe, Sane, and Consensual or Risk Aware Consensual Kink. If this is something that interests you, please make sure you know and trust your partner.

Although the characters in this book take part in consensual nonconsent, in real life this type of setup is quite rare. Even in short scenes the players discuss the matter in depth and still often have a safe word in place in case something goes wrong—because accidents happen even among the most experienced of kinksters.

Love, passion, and consensual kink are wonderful things as long as you play in safety with partners you know and trust.

Chapter One

"What the fuck have I gotten myself into?" Kyle Orion muttered through clenched teeth. A well-lit stage stood front and center of the room. A St. Andrew's Cross, a spanking bench, a table on a tilt frame, and a small table covered with a black cloth decorated the stage. "This is insane!" Dozens of men and woman mingled, laughing, chatting in low voices, some on their feet while others knelt at the side or feet of apparent Dominants.

Apparent was the word. Some were blatant posers. You only had to look at how they "handled" the submissives around them. Arrogance incarnate, strutting around the room and snapping orders at submissives who obviously weren't in their care, yet they still expected to be obeyed.

Losers.

You found them everywhere in chat rooms, e-mail groups, munches, lectures, and demos like this one and full-blown play events or clubs. There had been a rise in them, men and women who walked in and expected all those who identified as submissive to fall to their knees, willing to obey everything that the Dominant demanded of them. Not how it worked, but they'd learn that one the hard way. Kyle had witnessed one would-be Dominant escorted out of the event. The man hadn't gone quietly, but his protests and removal had toned down the worst of the behavior from others.

"Find somewhere to sit." Jake rested one hand lightly on Kyle's shoulder. "If you try hanging out in the shadows, you'll only draw attention to yourself."

"Yeah, okay." He nodded but didn't move. "Lot of people."

Jake smiled. "Mistress Lyn is well-respected in the local community. This isn't her first demo and info night with us. We sold out long before you contacted me. I had to call in a few favors to get you in." Jake met Kyle's gaze. "Don't blow this for me."

"Thanks, man, appreciated." Kyle owed Jake, but in their world, friends helped each other out. "Anytime you need something from

Take Down

me, you've got it." Blow it? No, that wasn't on his agenda. If the presenter, Mistress Lyn, was his target, he'd make a grab for her well away from the club.

"It's nothing. You've had my back time and again." Jake shrugged it off. "About time I had the chance to pay off at least one debt."

Kyle turned his attention back to the stage. Watching a target out in the open went against everything he'd ever been taught. Staking out a target required a low-key appearance, not pulling on leather pants, a chest halter, and leather cuffs. Shit, even finding cuffs that were comfortable to wear for more than twenty minutes had been something of a battle until he'd bitten the bullet and walked into a high-end sex shop that specialized in leatherwork and custom orders. Now here he was, walking around a group of kinksters in garb that marked him as a submissive, despite the fact that he never played the role in his personal life.

Kyle nudged Jake before walking past into the large room. *So not sitting at the front.* Kyle meandered out, trying to match the general pace that the other observers used, found a chair toward the back, and settled into it. At least back here it was unlikely that those on stage would be able to make out his face. Tension tightened his back and shoulders, and he breathed slowly, forcing his muscles to relax despite the situation. He'd already drawn unwanted attention from more than his fair share of the men and women in the room.

Well, if they approached him, he'd deal with it. Politely. An experienced Dominant or even a newbie who had taken the time to read the rules and do a little research into lifestyle would accept a refusal without raising a fuss. Fine, so the cuffs he'd chosen marked him as a submissive, but the rules were clear, and this wasn't a hook-up event.

Lighting changed, the main body of the room growing dim as spotlights focused on the stage. Conversation ceased, and those who had yet to find seats scurried to do so moments before a middle-aged man in black jeans and a simple black T-shirt walked out onto the stage, mic in hand.

"Ladies and gentleman, Dominants, switches, and submissives, welcome. As you know, we're fortunate to be able to welcome Mistress Lyn and her submissive, Bella. Mistress Lyn is well known as a professional Dominant, with a specialization in working with new submissives, helping them find their limits, understand their desires, and introducing them not only to the basics of physical play but the safety aspects of our world." He turned and waved toward the left hand side of the stage. "Please put your hands together to welcome Mistress Lyn and Bella."

Enthusiastic clapping rose from the audience, and Kyle added his own polite claps to the mix.

Two women strolled onto the stage, and Kyle let his gaze move to the second of them, the submissive. Slender and petite, with long, red-blonde hair and a sensual sway to her hips. This was so not the woman he was looking for.

Well, shit, this is a bust.

He scowled and leaned back in the chair, casting a quick look at the Dominant. Spiked black hair, a PVC cat suit with the zipper pulled down beneath her bra, exposing a tantalizing amount of cleavage, eight-inch spike heels, and an arrogant strut to her walk. Every inch the stereotypical pro Domme right off the pages of a porn site.

"Thank you." Mistress Lyn turned to face the crowd. "This is what you were expecting, right?" A cold, crisp voice carried easily to the back of the room.

A low, nervous chuckle rippled through the audience.

"All a part of the deal, when you hire a pro Domme, isn't it?" She gestured to the PVC cat suit. "Heels, suit, whip, and attitude! The real deal!" She reached for the curled single tail on her hip and slipped it out, letting the long length of braided leather unfurl. "An act, ladies and gentlemen, one I might put on for a client asking for a specific scene, but this is not how Mistress Lyn normally appears."

Confusion rumbled through the crowd.

Take Down

"No, in fact you wouldn't catch me dead in heels like that without a damned good reason." This time it wasn't the woman in PVC who spoke. Dressed in torn black jeans with long purple hair, a black sports-bra-like top, and black Darcy boots, the new speaker strode in from the right-hand side of the stage. "Personally, I'd rather be able to move, stretch—and yes, sweat—when I'm working with a submissive." With a brilliant smile made all the more unexpected by the black lipstick, the curvaceous woman with her full breasts and tempting curves turned to look out over the audience. Piercings glinted from multiple points in both ears, her left eyebrow, and left nostril. Curved over her right breast vanishing beneath the cover of her top was a tattoo of a raven.

Not the only tattoo either, from the brief glimpse he'd caught when the woman had entered the stage.

Kyle swore under his breath, his gaze locked on the Dominant who now commanded the stage.

Beneath all of the hair dye, tattoos, piercings and attitude, Mistress Lyn was his target.

* * * *

"I've heard you're the best at what you do, so I'd like you to find my sister, Mr. Orion." Cassandra Grant pushed the plain manila file across the desk. "And quickly."

"What's the rush?" Kyle leaned back in the chair, his jean legs stretched out in front of him, one booted foot crossed over the other at the ankle.

A pair of ice-blue eyes glinted back at him. "You weren't briefed?"

"Of course." He let his gaze move to the file and then back up to the woman on the opposite side of the desk. "But I want to hear it from you. I want to see the truth in your eyes before I agree." Recovery jobs were always dangerous in some way, shape, or form. Best-case scenario, you ran the risk of being arrested if the target wasn't a bail jumper, which was why such jobs were rarely accepted; worst case, they defended themselves in a way that put both

6

the hunter and the general public at risk.

She frowned; lines furrowed between her eyes and across her brow. "I don't understand. I signed the contract with Mr. Brent only yesterday." The soft Midwest tones did little to take the edge from her words. "Are you suggesting that—"

"I'm making it clear that I might refuse the job." He cut through her words. "And then Mr. Brent will assign someone else from the team." He kept his voice calm, fingers interlinked across his stomach, his elbows resting on the arms of the chair. Cassandra flinched as he continued. Harvey Brent ran a top-class team, and the small group of seven men and women who worked for him had become a second family to Kyle. "Why is it so important to you that your sister is returned home? She's an adult, with her own life and choices ahead of her, wouldn't you agree?"

"Yes." Cassandra pushed her chair back and rose, shaking her head as the tension eased from her shoulders. Soft wisps curled down from a harsh bun that her hair had been scraped into. The style wasn't flattering, but this was a woman who understood what it was like to sit on the control side of the desk. Her voice took on a softer tone, one that didn't quite match the image she had tried, only a moment before, to portray. "She's an adult, but this isn't just about her, Mr. Orion. This is about family. If she doesn't return, then that woman, my father's second wife, will get her hands on everything my father has built." Cassandra paused, strain furrowing her brow. "I'll be honest with you. This is about protecting a legacy. All my sister has to do is come home and sign the papers. Hell, if anyone understands why she left, why she wouldn't want anything to do with the family, it's me, but I can't let that gold-digging bitch of a second wife get her hands on all of this." She gestured to the well placed office. "Maybe Carolyn will stay, maybe we'll be able to fix this thing between us. I don't know." She shrugged and rubbed her temples with slender, well-manicured fingers. "I've heard almost nothing from her since the day she stormed out of this very room on our eighteenth birthday." She sighed and walked away

Take Down

from the desk.

Cassandra Grant was, without a doubt, an attractive woman but lacked the confidence that should have come with both her family's wealth and her beauty. Kyle smiled. Oh, she had learned to play the part well enough, at least to those who didn't know how to read body language and look for those little signs that might give away what was going on with her.

He let his gaze move over her, assessing her. Pale skin, high forehead, brilliant eyes, and near white-blonde hair, full breasts and hips, with a waist that begged for a man's hand. A well-tailored dark blue pantsuit matched with low heels and a simple pair of gold earrings completed her businesslike appearance. She wasn't a slender beauty but strong and still very feminine; she moved with a cautious step, with eyes that only briefly met his. A soft beauty with hidden edges beneath the surface.

"And if she doesn't want to return with me?" He didn't move, didn't shift from what he knew to be an insolent position, considering it was her office. He kept his voice soft, adding a drawl to his words and his gaze never left the woman before him. "What do you want me to do when I explain everything to her, lay out the problems in front of her, and she tells me to go to hell?"

Cassandra pushed back her shoulders, set her jaw, and closed the gap between them. She leaned down, slender fingers wrapped around the arms of the chair, her face inches away from his. All softness vanished, an edge in her clipped words. "You bring her back. I don't care if you have to toss her over your damned shoulder! You handcuff her stubborn ass and bring her back here, kicking and screaming if need be. Is that clear, Mr. Orion?"

* * * *

Mistress Lyn.

Kyle's gaze narrowed on the young woman with her long purple hair. How often did she have to dye it in order to keep the bold color? Was it just to hide her appearance, or was this part of a full-blown rebellion against her background? His gaze narrowed as he

8

took in the assorted piercings and tattoos. The woman wasn't exactly what he'd expected, especially after meeting Cassandra of the perfect suit and carefully tended hair. Cassandra had portrayed a near perfect example of a businesswoman from a well-placed family.

He frowned, going over the meeting, freezing a mental image of Cassandra. Yes, there'd been a simple pair of gold earrings. Just enough to draw attention to Cassandra's ears without throwing wealth and position in his face. Smart woman. So, what was Carolyn's plan here? An act? A means of hiding in plain view? No, pretending to be a pro Domme didn't get you invited to clubs and groups like this one to run a demo or lecture. That required both actual skill and knowledge. Not something easily faked.

Intelligence, beauty, and sexual confidence. What other interesting traits did she have?

It doesn't matter. Not like I'm here to get to know her. This is a grab and return, not a first-date situation.

The woman moved across the stage, head held high, her voice carrying to the back of the hall. "Fantasies are all well and good, but the reality is that we dress how we feel comfortable. In clothing that allows us freedom of movement. Not that I haven't pulled on the odd fetish dress from time to time, a corset, heels, or even a mask, but when I'm working with someone who knows me, this is my preferred garb." She gestured to the jeans and low boots. "Let's be honest, jeans are a damn sight easier to get in and out of than a leather fetish dress or a PVC cat suit. Cheaper too! Even a pro has to watch the bank account. The job doesn't exactly come with a retirement bonus."

A few chuckles and grunts of approval rose from the audience before she continued, moving into the demo part of the night.

Able to laugh at herself—nice touch. He followed every move. She was skilled, that was obvious from the first time she picked up a crop. Her tools were top quality and well cared for, her explanations were clear, and when she answered a question she did so without preaching to her audience. Within a few minutes, she had the majority of the audience eating out of her hand.

And this is the woman I'm expected to bring to heel if she proves problematic? This wasn't someone who would go without a fight, a thought confirmed when she went over basic self-defense. Lyn, or rather Carolyn, didn't pull punches. In between working with Bella, she went over both best-case and worst-case scenarios, what a Dominant's emergency box should contain—from first aid to a good pair of scissors and a knife to cut through restraints, advising that a bolt cutter should be kept on hand if chains were a part of the scene.

"There's nothing more embarrassing than having to call in emergency services or a locksmith in order to free your partner. Keep spare keys and bolt cutters on hand! But if you find yourself in a bind, make sure you have a good explanation or you're calling someone you trust."

"What if you don't have a good explanation, and they call in the cops?" a young woman yelled out. "I mean, what do you do then?"

"Good question. You stay calm, smile, and answer their questions. Keep it simple and keep to the truth. Harder to keep track of lies and easier to make a mistake if they press you." Mistress Lyn set down the paddle she'd been using on the Bella, a slight smile touching her lips. "With all that in mind, I suggest you have a lawyer you can call. One who knows your interest in the lifestyle and is up to date on the current laws." Her ice-blue gaze swept over the room. "Many of us enjoy the forced seduction scenario, or mock rape, but we understand it's a game. One we've consented to well in advance. But remember, perception is reality, and in the heat of the moment you might find yourself charged with assault, rape, or even kidnap. Have your consent forms within easy reach, especially if you're playing with someone you don't have a long-standing history with. The forms won't save you but might be taken into account once your partner is able to explain their side of the situation."

Smart, articulate, able to deal with potential issues, all of which added up to problems for the man who might have to snatch her. He shook his head. Forget might, this was a woman who had, without a doubt, kept an eye on her family. A woman who was capable of teaching about the dangers of a scene, down to the paperwork side of things, would have watched her family, tracked them, if for no other reason than to know if they came looking for her. Between search engine alerts and online newspapers, she would have been well informed. If she didn't know her father was dead, Kyle was a flying monkey.

Which also meant she had no desire to return home. Had she wanted to, Lyn would have returned for the funeral. No, if his instincts were correct then Mistress Lyn would return home either the hard way, or not at all.

Well, shit.

Chapter Two

"You did well out there, my girl." Carolyn tucked a soft blanket around Bella's shoulders and slipped her arm down to the submissive's waist, supporting her as they walked off the stage. Bella leaned into her. "You'll need to rest, and we can get you into a warm shower once you're steady on your feet."

"Thank you, ma'am." Bella flushed, lowering her gaze, a soft tremor moving through her body. Her voice was breathy, and she licked her bottom lip before continuing. "Ma'am, I was so pleased that you wanted me for the demo. I know you had a lot of others you could have turned to. Men and women who would have looked better on the stage, perhaps given more of a show. I can't explain how thrilled and honored I was. Still am... Sorry, I'm babbling."

Carolyn smiled and patted the girl on the shoulder before stepping back and giving her a once-over. Flushed cheeks, a soft look in the eyes, a shine that spoke of excitement—there were other signs, of course, but they all spoke of the emotions Bella had endured on stage, along with the physical side of the scene. The young woman's eyes glistened, her pupils slightly dilated. Her focus was off and would remain so for a time. Scenes took a lot out of both the Dominant and submissive. They were the kinky equivalent of both a mental and physical workout. *How many outside of the scene would ever understand or even begin to believe that?*

"Babbling is to be expected, little one. As for others I could have chosen, maybe that's true, but I prefer to work with submissives who give themselves for the sake of the scene, not for their own desires. Someone who knows that I'm going to have to pause now and then in order to explain something to the audience."

"Well, I guess when you pay for something..." Bella's blush deepened. "Sorry, ma'am. I didn't mean to offend. You're not exactly the have flogger, will travel type."

Carolyn chuckled at the flogger comment—now there was a tag she could see on a T-shirt. "You didn't; you spoke the truth.

Nothing more, nothing less. I don't ever punish a sub for speaking the truth. If I can't handle the words, then it's time for me to get out of this business." She stroked three fingers over the girl's cheek before she shook her head and listened. The low murmur from the audience had returned after a deafening round of applause at the end of the demonstration. It hadn't been her best performance, but it had worked. If she helped prevent one Dom from making a mistake, one sub from rushing into a bad situation, then it was worth every ounce of discomfort Carolyn had experienced up on that stage. "Besides, you've just been through a hectic scene and get a small pass on anything that stumbles out of those sweet lips." She released her grip on Bella, turning to face her.

"Thank you, ma'am." Fresh heat turned Bella's cheeks crimson as she lowered her gaze, head dipping down.

Bella kept her head down until Carolyn forced two fingers under the young woman's chin, silently commanding Bella to lift her gaze. "You don't need to lower your gaze with me, girl. It's rare that I require such a thing and never outside of a scene." *Bloody stupid habit, if you ask me. Need to see the eyes in order to keep track of the sub's mental well-being.* Oh, Carolyn knew why some Dominants insisted on it, why it was a common training practice, and why it was a perceived expectation when it came to interactions between a Dom and a sub, but it didn't mean she had to agree with it. *How many bad situations have I managed to avoid because I watched for changes in expressions?* More than she wanted to think about.

"I understand." The young woman smiled, took a deep breath and met Carolyn's gaze. Bella's eyes widened, nostrils flared, and a shiver claimed her body. She leaned in, drawing closer to Carolyn before she corrected her posture. "Do you need me further, ma'am? I'm a little shaky," Bella inquired.

"No, let's get you somewhere safe." Carolyn waved at two of the assistants the club had offered her. "Sandra, Blake, if you could help Bella here." Normally she'd see to the complete aftercare herself, but the club had insisted she make herself available to the

Take Down

audience after the demo. She gave Bella a once-over, checking for any sign of danger, an injury she might have missed, but there was nothing more than the woman's standard reactions of shakes. A warm blanket, water, and a small amount of chocolate would have Bella settled. If there were any problems, either Sandra or Blake would come to find her.

"Yes, Mistress Lyn. She'll be safe in our hands." Sandra smiled and moved next to Bella. "We have the list you provided, and there's hot chocolate being prepared."

Of that Carolyn had no doubt. "Thank you. Just remember, don't let her fall asleep." Without someone Bella knew to hold her if she slept, there was a high risk of nightmares. Something she'd learned the hard way with this particular submissive.

Jake made his way through the small group at the side of the stage. "Are you ready, Mistress Lyn?"

"Just Lyn." She turned to greet the man. "And yes I'm ready." Jake. Decent man, firm but willing to bend on a few things. At first, he hadn't liked the idea of the fake Lyn, but when she'd explained her reasoning, he'd accepted it and worked with her. "Many out there?"

"Most of them," Jake admitted, a warm smile touching his eyes. "You made quite an impact on the group. Impressive."

That had been the plan. "Glad to hear it all worked out." *Lots of new members, which is why they asked me back.* Well, if her little act had shaken a few people up, then so much the better. "They seem like a decent lot." At least, most of them did. She hadn't missed the one man being escorted out.

"The regulars are, and they were smart enough not to let on that your double was a fake. As for the guests, that can always be hit or miss." Jake gestured toward the auditorium. "Shall we?"

"Indeed." She patted a loose strand of hair back into place and followed him out past the curtains. How many had been out there in the audience? A hundred? Maybe more. It had been hard to tell from her place on the stage.

Her throat tightened. Over a hundred people still waited for her. Some in jeans and T-shirts, others in fetish gear that ranged from the mild to the wild. Businessmen who played the game, women in skimpy outfits with collars or loose chains around their necks, and everything in between. A band tightened around her heart, and sweat beaded down the length of her back as she stopped. Breathe, she had to breathe and let the panic ease. They weren't judging her. They didn't know her background and sure as hell weren't trying to use her to get to her father or the company. No, they wanted to talk, to get to know her, to find out how she could help them. There would be a few submissives who would offer themselves, those who hadn't heard a word she had said and had been focused on her actions and how she had made Bella dance beneath the touch of crop, lash, and paddle.

They were drawn to the danger of submission, eager to offer themselves, and too emotionally young to think beyond the moment.

We were all that way, once. Willing to dive into the deep, dark end without thinking it through. God, how close to the edge did I come before I realized how dangerous it all was?

She'd be the first to admit, if asked outright, that she'd made some damned stupid mistakes early on. If anything, that added to her desire to shake the ones who would kneel and plead for a chance with her. They knew better. They were here, they'd read the rules, had a chance to talk to others who had more experience, but that didn't stop the rush, either the sub or Dom version. That dangerous drive to push the boundaries, explore, and then jump off the cliff regardless of the danger.

"Mistress Lyn, thank you for doing this. I can't tell you what an honor it was to—"

"Just Lyn." She smiled at the eager young woman who moved toward her as she walked into the auditorium. Carolyn was a name she never used with those in the scene as it increased the chances of someone tracing her to her home address on the edge of Las

Take Down

Vegas.

"Pardon?" The bubbly, brown haired, slender woman frowned.

"When I'm not in a scene, I'm just like everyone else. Lyn works fine." Carolyn continued. "I'm not your Mistress, and this isn't a formal full-service event." She winked, trying to take the sting from her words. "Many Dominants will be flattered by the offer of the title but will tell you the same thing. Titles are for your Dominant, not for every Tom, Dick, or Lyn—otherwise they become meaningless. Those who insist on the titles at all times, those are the ones you want to be a little wary of. Some have good reason, and some have earned it being a whip master or skilled toy maker; others are posers trying to enforce their *rank* on you."

Color claimed the woman's features, and she shifted her weight awkwardly from one foot to the other. "I'm sorry. I didn't think about it that way. It's just that— I mean, online they—"

"Chat rooms are great for exploring ideas, but they're fantasy. No one can force you to your knees through a computer screen. If you don't like what's going on, you can hit Leave or X out of the room. In real life you should go by the rules of the event or club. I believe, if you read the information about this club, it goes over expected protocols." Chat rooms, online groups, and message boards were all fine when you were trying to figure things out, but unless you balanced that with common sense, you ran the risk of coming out thinking that you knelt to every Dominant, had no limits, and whatever other myths you wanted to include in the mix. Oh, it wasn't that such relationships didn't exist, but tempering fantasy with reality was the only safe way to go in Lyn's mind.

"So, you don't have a problem with people exploring online?" A strong, deep male voice with a hint of humor broke through the background noise.

Carolyn turned her attention away from the young woman to meet the hazel gaze of a tall, black-haired man in leather pants, and a chest harness complete with a heavy, stainless steel chain around his neck and leather cuffs locked at his wrists. She swallowed but tried to hide the reaction, refusing to look away from the powerful gaze that drilled into her. "No, I don't. There are some good resources that can be found online. In some respects, it can be a safe environment when you're taking the first steps in figuring out if this is for you or not." Need, hard and unrelenting, moved through her body, down from her chest, tightening her nipples and breasts, into her jeans until damp, clenching hunger coated her inner walls.

"You don't like online resources?" The female submissive turned her attention to the interloper, searching his face for answers. "They can be a good start, as Mistress Lyn said. I don't understand—"

He moved closer, cutting her off with a graceful, dangerous prowl that put the woman within grabbing range. "I never said that." His voice dropped into a low purr. He leaned in, not enough to infringe on the woman's space, his gaze narrowing, locked on the submissive. "It's not wise to put words into someone else's mouth."

The *little one* or *girl* was missing from the statement, but his tone, the way he looked at the submissive, spoke volumes. *Powerful, and he knows how to use it in order to control people. Damn. If he's a submissive, I'm going to put in an order for flying monkeys.*

"I'm sorry," the young woman stammered. "I didn't mean to offend." The woman's gaze automatically lowered.

Fuck, if he growls at her, she'll be on her knees in a heartbeat.

He shifted his weight, left hand moving, and for a moment Carolyn wondered if he was about to reach out and cup the woman's chin or touch her cheek. Then the moment vanished, and he turned his attention away from the submissive to pin Carolyn with the full force of his gaze. "My apologies, I didn't mean to barge into the middle of a conversation." His tone changed from the subtle power she had felt before to one far less confident.

Fake, so not buying it. Her sex clenched as their eyes locked. Heat, need, hunger, it didn't matter what she called it. The effect claimed her, threatening to leave her panties moist and her heart racing. She bit back a snarl and forced a calm smile into place. He

Take Down

couldn't know. No way would she let this bastard know that he affected her. Not like this. "Not a problem. These after-demo talks are always informal. I find the informality allows for a better flow of conversation and information. Otherwise a lot of submissives will look to the Dominants to lead the conversation. Some are even wary about speaking out at all." *Hazel eyes, gold flecks, a strong jaw, and dark hair cut short. A military cut? No, not quite, close though.* Dark stubble shadowed his jaw and top lip, though not from poor grooming.

Intentional?

Strong build not too muscled. He wasn't a gym rat. No, this was a man who worked out to keep himself in shape. *For his work or a habit from time in the military?* His stance, the way he watched the room, he was aware of everything and everyone around him.

Why is he here?

"Thank you for your understanding, Lyn." He flashed a grin, and her gaze was drawn to a small chip in his top left canine. A tiny imperfection that drew her in, making her want to study him further. "Not all Mistresses are so forgiving."

"During a scene, I'm not." She returned the smile even as she made the decision to draw a line in the sand. "Not that you'll ever get the chance to find out."

Not a line, a fucking wall. Ten feet high, topped with razor wire. No way in hell I'm ever doing a scene with this one!

A CHALLENGE. WELL, you have to like a woman who knows what she wants and where to draw the line, Kyle mused.

A line she had now drawn in a very public way. Carolyn Grant wouldn't be an easy woman to bring in, but he'd be damned if he was going to walk away from this job. Not when the prize was standing right in front of him, issuing a challenge he couldn't turn his back on.

Mistress Lyn was curvaceous, somewhere between a size sixteen and eighteen, depending on the cut of the clothing. She wasn't shy either. There'd been no attempt to throw on an overshirt or even a T-shirt before she'd stepped out into the audience. She had full breasts, strong, good muscle tone, and killer legs. He couldn't help but wonder what they would look like in high heels, though she'd made her distaste about heels damned clear.

If she were mine I'd have her in heels, if only once, and she wouldn't be walking around in them. Heels, stockings, and old-fashioned garters.

His cock thickened at the thought, balls tight as he let his gaze move slowly over the woman in front of him. Hunger claimed him, and for a moment he debated reaching out and touching her. His shoulders tensed as he made sure his hands remained at his sides. What the hell was he thinking? This was his target, not a woman he was trying to pick up at a bar or a club. That meant she was off limits. Completely.

Yet the thought of her naked except for those heels...

"What if I tried to hire your services?"

"I have the final say on who I take on as clients. A fact you would do well to remember." Carolyn arched an eyebrow before she deliberately turned her attention back to the submissive woman who had begun the conversation.

Mistress Lyn is one stubborn woman. Then again, she'd have to be in her line of work. A woman who worked as a pro Domme who was easy to push around would quickly find herself out of business or worse, a victim in a crime report. No, this one knew how to handle situations. Better yet, she knew who was too dangerous to scene with, which meant approaching her as a potential client as a means of snatching her wasn't happening.

Would there be a chance at getting her to return home of her own free will?

He frowned as he watched the woman, the way she spoke to others, her confidence and grace. No. If she'd ever wanted to return to Minnesota, she'd have already done so. The file had been clear. She was in occasional contact with her sister, Cassandra, using anonymous e-mail, taking care to cover her tracks. Any time the

Take Down

twin in Minnesota brought up the idea of Carolyn visiting, the idea had been slapped down, and contact had ended for a time only to begin again using yet another e-mail.

No, this wouldn't be an easy *let's have a quick chat and go home* job.

He watched Lyn for a little longer before he slipped back through the crowd, making his way to the side of the room. There, in the shadows, he leaned against the wall, observing his target: the woman who tempted him with licks of flame that made their way up and down his spine. Beautiful, strong, confident—everything a woman should be, and yet she didn't match conventional ideas of beauty. Her chin was a little too strong. The color of her hair and the multiple piercings spoke of rebellion, a bad girl, one his palm itched to correct. An act she used as a shield, or was this the real Lyn?

How would she take to a spanking? He smiled. He'd have to hold her in place. She'd fight, kick, maybe even bite, but then there come a moment when she'd surrender to him. It wouldn't be permanent, nor would she seek out a man to submit to. No, that surrender would be willingly torn from her.

What the hell! That doesn't happen—it's insane.

But it did. Consensual nonconsent wasn't unheard of, but it was a rare couple that took part in such a thing. He'd seen takedown scenes, which were a form of consensual nonconsent. Those fights, which they were for all intents and purposes, involved the Dominant or Dominants taking the submissive down to the ground, forcing them to submit. Some then bound their prize; others took the submissive there and then, but that was all worked out, agreed to beforehand. Would Mistress Lyn ever agree to such a scene?

Would she agree to it with him, with Lyn taking on the role of the submissive?

Not only no, but hell no.

His partners had, before this, all been willing submissives or switches who had come to him to explore the submissive side to their nature. Neither described the woman he watched cut a path through the crowd. With Carolyn, that was the only way she would ever submit: if it was taken from her, earned by a stronger Dominant. His target was, without a doubt, a Dominant, and only with the right man or woman would she ever submit. The submission wouldn't be permanent, but a moment where she let the walls down, surrendered deeply, and let another take control. Once that moment was over and done with, all hell would break loose. She'd fight, kick, push back, and try to put him on his knees. She'd have to in order to regain herself, to keep her confidence.

With him she'd find a man who wouldn't kneel, no matter what she tried, but the fight, the struggle... He groaned at the thought and adjusted his straining, rebellious cock. The idea thrilled and terrified him in the same breath, and damn if he didn't want to experience the entire thing.

Take Down

Chapter Three

"Well, that was a bust," Carolyn muttered and turned the car around in order to begin the journey home. "Waste of time and gas." She glanced in her rearview mirror as she left. Despite an e-mail letting her know that her order for a new whip was ready, when she'd driven to the Whip Master's house, the man hadn't been there. Nor had there been any sign that he'd been there all day, which didn't make sense.

"Where the fuck is he?" she muttered, rolled out her shoulders, and tried to focus on driving. Given Master Tim's reputation, this wasn't like him. She'd bought items from him before, and he'd always been reliable until now. Sure, the man didn't like mailing items out, but that was a matter of professional pride and a desire to see the finished product in the hands of the one who'd ordered it.

Fine, so it was more than professional pride. The Whip Master checked the fit of the item, making any small corrections that might be needed. Something that couldn't be done if the item was mailed out.

Maybe there'd been a technical issue? An e-mail sent out with the wrong time and date on it? Human error?

Well, shit happened, and making a fuss over it wasn't worth the effort.

With everything that had occurred and kept her on her toes since the demo three days earlier, it was surprising that she knew her own name. Her computer had done its update routine, only to then spiral into a twenty-four-hour spin of restart, refuse to work correctly, and then restart again.

Jake from the club had called to let her know that the man who'd been removed from the event had made threats against both the club and Carolyn, which had led her to double-checking her home security. That in turn had revealed a few things out of place but not enough to set off major alarms. After all, they were small things outside of her house, like the stone dragon at the side of the door—and she couldn't be certain if that had been moved or it was just a figment of her imagination.

Then she'd opened her e-mail, and her world had changed.

He's dead. It was going to happen sooner or later. I just never...

She gave herself a shake, but knowledge and grief clenched her heart, refusing to release their shared grip. Any hope she had held out that there would one day be peace between herself and her father had shattered with the news of his passing.

He wouldn't have forgiven me. In his eyes, I betrayed him. I turned my back on everything he had built, his plans for me, and the marriage he would have tried to force me into.

That didn't help, didn't stop the tears that threatened to spill. Yes, she had ceased to be the dutiful daughter, but the reality of it was that she'd never been the good twin. That had been Cassandra's role. So why did it hurt so much? Carolyn blinked, clearing her vision. The decision to run—and she refused to lie to herself about that—had been the right one. If she'd stayed, her life would never have been her own. The man her father had been before the bitch queen had walked into his life would have understood that.

Tension tightened the muscles across her shoulders. Their lives had changed for the worse when their father had remarried. Everything that had made their father the good man, the caring man, the one that Carolyn could turn to, had vanished in the years after that damned ceremony. Perhaps she couldn't blame the change entirely on his decision. No one had forced him to treat his daughters as marriage bait, yet she hadn't seen any sign of the darker, cold-hearted man until he had welcomed that woman into their lives.

"Focus on the bloody road," she grumbled, forcing her way through the fog of emotions. "No point in getting myself killed." Not that there were any other cars on the road, but that didn't rule out wildlife. Deer weren't likely to run out in front of the car out here, but that didn't mean there weren't other animals out there, such as pronghorns, bobcats, coyotes, and a dozen other critters

Take Down

large enough to cause damage or make her to swerve off the road.

The distant lights of Mountain Springs beckoned, though she wouldn't be back in what she considered home turf until she saw the lights of Vegas. There were parts of the road where she couldn't see more than the faintest glow of lights from either Mountain Springs or Las Vegas. Not that it mattered. She knew this road well enough, having visited Master Tim several times at his home. In truth, he was one of the few local male Dominants she felt comfortable around. He'd never made a move on her, nor disparaged her profession, something that was sadly often commonplace. That, and his skill with leather, creating single tails and floggers, was among the reasons why she referred to him as Master.

The single tail he'd created for her in black, red, and white, was a work of art. From the first time she'd held it, felt the braided handle against the palm of her hand, she'd known that Master Tim was the only one she'd ever order leather goods from again. He'd measured her grip before beginning his work. Hell, he'd measured her palm, length of her arm, and her height, adjusting his notes after he'd watched her work with three different single tails of his own design.

He didn't make generic toys; he'd told her that from the beginning.

A soft, odd noise vibrated from beneath the hood of her car. She frowned, listening for the sound, only to hear it again. A soft shudder worked through the vehicle, dying off before it repeated twice more. Each time the tremors increased, and with it a soft coughing sound from the exhaust. "That doesn't sound good."

How far away from Mountain Springs was she? Five miles maybe? Her jaw clenched as she nursed the car. If she could reach civilization, she could find help easily enough. If nothing else, there was the bar or the fire station. In truth the town was a tiny one, but it was better than nothing at all.

The car shuddered and groaned, jerking forward hard enough to shake her, slamming her head toward the steering wheel. She braced just in time, her back and neck protesting, but it wasn't enough to set off the airbags. Swearing under her breath, Carolyn eased off to the side of the road.

"Come on, baby. Don't do this to me. We're not that far from home." Not entirely a lie, but the car was a good one and had never let her down before. Her jaw clenched. What was wrong with the damned thing? She'd taken it in for a service only ten days ago, and nothing had come up on the report.

Had they missed something?

"Keep it together a little longer, at least until we reach the bar. It'll all work out." The car protested, surged once despite being at the side of the road, and then died. "No. Come on! Don't do this to me." Nothing happened. She stared at the dashboard, turned the key again, trying to restart the car, only to be rewarded with a momentary stutter before the lights flickered and died, matching the death of the engine. With a growl she smacked the steering wheel, tried again, and then resorted to swearing. The car remained stubbornly dark and silent by the side of the road. "No, not here."

Carolyn reached for her cell phone, turning on the screen only to swear again. No bars. "This isn't happening to me. Not here. Not now." She turned, twisting in the seat, lifting the phone first one way and then the other in an attempt to find a single bar. "Come on, one bar, just give me one." The phone, of course, didn't respond. She swore, threatening the phone with being smashed on the ground, stomped on, and anything else that might work. A foolish reaction, something she acknowledged even as she did it, but that didn't prevent her from trying several times before giving up.

"I don't need this shit. Not today," she mumbled before she twisted and reached back, tugging out the small emergency bag she kept in the car. A few minutes later she had her flashlight in hand. "Hah, this isn't Minnesota." She checked the flashlight and grinned. Sure, Las Vegas was an interesting place, but with the variety of people who visited came a level of wariness that seeped into everyday life. You might get an offer to call in for help, but some-

Take Down

one actually getting out of a car to assist you was another matter entirely.

A back road in the middle of nowhere Nevada. Could there possibly be a worse location to be stuck at the side of the road, on her own, at night?

"The middle of a city, near the biggest dive bar in existence. Yup, that could be worse." Still muttering under her breath, Carolyn switched on the flashlight, grabbed her purse, stuck a bottle of water in the top of the purse, and stepped out of the car, checking the ground for any sign of snakes. She shuddered at the thought of the nasty things. Oh, she wasn't afraid of them, not exactly, but she sure as hell had a healthy respect for the danger they posed. Still, with the nightly drop in temperatures, the chances of running into one were reduced, but it wasn't a risk she wanted to take. She'd have a better chance of waving down a car instead of being run over by one if she kept the flashlight switched on. For a moment she debated on lifting the hood and checking the engine but dismissed the idea. She wasn't a mechanic, and even if she found something that looked wrong, she didn't know what to do. Changing a tire was one thing, but messing with an engine that even a mechanic needed a computer to check was another.

She locked her car, checking the doors and windows before turning in the direction of town. Worst-case scenario, she had a potentially grueling walk ahead of her; best case, someone would drive past within a couple of minutes and pick her up.

She swept the beam of the flashlight back and forth across the surface of the road, checking for potential problems as she walked.

"All right, so maybe this isn't so bad." A walk would clear her head and give her time to think. She still hadn't processed everything that had happened at the demo. Fine, so she wasn't having to work through a mess of emotions or problems. Bella had been wonderful, and the event had been a success, but there was still that one male submissive that lingered in the back of her mind.

Carolyn shivered and caught her bottom lip between her teeth.

His build, the way he'd approached her, spoken to her and the young woman at the event. Despite the chain around his neck that had suggested he was a submissive, his demeanor declared otherwise in a mile-high sign in lime-green letters pasted over his head, and her body had responded to that dominant presence.

She didn't have to close her eyes in order to see him again. Strong, chiseled but athletic. The type that spoke of a man of action rather than a muscled beach body. No, that was a man who knew how to fight, to move, and the danger that clung to his form was yet another reason why she was going to stay as far away from him as possible.

Yet she wanted him. Her nipples hardened at the memory, her breasts tight even as her inner walls clenched, threatening to coat with liquid heat. She swallowed hard, her body hungry for something only he would be able to give her, even as she accepted that this was a man she had to stay away from. His touch would devastate; she knew that without experiencing it. This was a man who would challenge her, try to bring her to her knees, and—for a moment—she might be tempted to let the walls down.

"So not going there. I don't do Doms. Not unless they want to experience the other end of the whip." She groaned, trying to push the image out of her mind. "I'm not a submissive. Nope. Not my thing. Not even with one like him."

One step in front of the other, that was all she had to keep doing. One step, one more, and another. Each step would bring her closer to the town and help. The soft glow beckoned her, and after a time, her thoughts turned away from the dangerous unknown man from the club to other matters. Her home, the life she'd carved out for herself in Vegas. It hadn't been easy, but leaving her family and Minnesota behind had been the right thing.

He's dead. This isn't the time or place to think about him.

God alone knew that her father had done everything he could to make her stay. Right down to cutting her off and taking back the car that was in his name. Fortunately, she'd planned ahead—two years

Take Down

of planning, to be exact. Small jobs, hiding a fraction of her weekly allowance, and building up a network of friends. He'd still tried to find her, but when she'd left, she'd been eighteen, and there was nothing that he could do to stop her. At least, nothing legal.

Bastard.

Okay, maybe that wasn't the right thing to call her dad. He'd been decent once, before the bitch queen had walked into his life.

"No way I'm ever going back there. They can both burn for all I care." The only thing she regretted was leaving Cassandra behind. "Damnit, Cassandra, you could have come with me, but no, you had to stay with Daddy." Carolyn kicked at a small loose rock in her way, sending it skittering across the road before it disappeared from sight. "We'd have been fine together. So what if he would have then given the business to that damned woman! I didn't care; you shouldn't have either."

Stop it.

The past was done, the future lay ahead of her, and she was never going to look back.

She paused, glancing at her feet, letting the flashlight pause in the back and forth across the road. "Well, what's done is done. No going back now. Cassandra's happy. She must be or she'd have gotten the hell out of there."

Strong arms wrapped around her from behind, one around her waist, the other around her neck, silencing her, cutting off her ability to scream even as her attacker lifted her from the ground. She kicked, twisting, clawing her nails into the arm around her neck. Breathe. She had to breathe, to calm down and break the hold. Somewhere within the back of her mind she recognized what was happening to her. A chokehold. Her pulse raced, pounding in her temples, pressure turning into pain as she fought, her heels slamming into the legs of her attacker.

I'm not going to be a victim. Won't let it happen.

Even as the darkness closed in around her, she kept repeating that mantra until the final edges of darkness claimed her and pulled her into its unforgiving embrace.

* * * *

Kyle stuck to the protection offered by the night and watched the slow approach of Lyn's flashlight. The beam swung back and forth as she walked away from the now-dead car. He grinned and rubbed his fingers over the kill switch in his top pocket. The small box was a nifty toy, and it wasn't the first time he'd used such a thing in order to bring a target's car to a sudden stop.

"No way I'm ever going back there. They can both burn for all I care." The woman's voice reached out through the dark as she walked. "Damnit, Cassandra, you could have come with me, but no, you had to stay with Daddy." She kicked at something, maybe a rock, sending it darting across the road with a clatter that rang through the night. "We'd have been fine together. So what if he would have then given the business to that damned woman! I didn't care; you shouldn't have either!"

Well, if he'd ever had any doubts about his choice, those words stripped them away. The anger and frustration were damned clear, and he didn't want to be in the room when the two sisters were reunited. Odds were, however, that he'd have to be present if for no other reason than to make sure that Carolyn didn't attempt to escape.

He'd been careful. He'd watched her for the past three days and sought information from people who had known her, using chat rooms that were favored by groups in the Vegas area. Trying to per-suade her was a lost cause. If given the choice, Carolyn Grant would tell him to go to hell and never come back. *There's more to this than Cassandra let on, but isn't that the norm?* No case was ever cut and dried, but that wasn't his problem. The woman was his target, and this wouldn't be the first time he'd taken part in a snatch and grab.

Except he'd never been involved in what was, if he wanted to be technical, a kidnapping. He frowned as he went over what he'd have to do. Subdue, restrain, and get out of there. She'd be tied up, helpless and... For a moment he could see it, her soft eyes looking

29

up at him, body arched, a silent plea for his touch. No, he wasn't going there. He swallowed hard even as his cock punched at the inside of his pants. Would she moan, look up at him, and silently beg for his touch, or would she continue to fight, to resist, despite what they both wanted? Oh, he wouldn't touch her, not until she begged. Consent would be there without a shadow of a doubt. Takedown scenes were one thing; rape was another game entirely.

Therein lay the problem: he was a professional, always would be, no matter how tempting the target might be, which meant what he wanted, what his body craved when he thought about Carolyn, couldn't happen.

Kyle closed his eyes for a count of three, just long enough to bring his rebellious body back under control before he opened them and watched the progress made by his walking temptation.

Target, not temptation. Get that straight. Keep things simple.

Easier said than done with the way his body reacted to her presence, still the KISS rule was something he had always embraced up until this point. KISS: Keep it simple, stupid. How many times had he heard that growing up?

The lack of streetlights was a bonus, easier to move in on her, but she'd fight. The strike had to be perfect or close to it in order to work without causing her serious harm. There'd be some bruises, but this was safer than using a drug, be it something in a drink or a dart. He didn't have access to her medical history, didn't know if there would be an interaction with something she was already taking or a medical condition he knew nothing about.

Silent, placing each step with care, he eased through the scrub and rocks toward the woman. If something shifted beneath his feet, even if he was certain he hadn't made a sound, he froze.

She was still muttering as she moved level with him and then passed. Only then did he make his way to the edge of the road, using the cover of a low, gnarled tree. If she turned to look back, the shadow provided by the tree should be enough to protect him from being seen.

Carolyn paused with her flashlight, and she sighed. "Well, what's done is done. No going back now. Cassandra's happy. She must be or she'd have gotten the hell out of there."

He moved, stepping up behind her, one arm around her throat, the other around her body as he lifted her up from the ground. The flashlight hit the ground, spinning and rolling until it stopped several feet away. He'd deal with that later. Right now he had a wild cat in his grasp. Pressure, he had to be careful with the pressure. Too much and he could crush her throat, too little and she wouldn't pass out. She struggled, kicking, twisting in his grip. Nails found the arm that he'd wrapped around her throat, sharp points that dug into his flesh, but he didn't give up. The choke hold was the fastest, safest way of knocking her out by cutting off the blood supply to her brain.

Damn it, stop fighting. I don't want to hurt you. He'd never wanted to hurt her. Not unless she wanted it. A spanking, flogging, a single tail or paddle across her ass. He shook his head, trying to force those thoughts to the back of his mind. Not the time. Not the place. He kept silent, holding her as she fought. *Say nothing, in case someone hears it.* There was no one else around, but it wasn't a risk he was willing to take.

She clawed, heels slamming back against his shins. He'd have bruises come the morning. Ones well earned.

The struggles eased, growing weaker with each second until she passed out, becoming limp in his arms. He eased up on his grip, checking her pulse and breathing before he laid her down on the road long enough to collect the flashlight. Only then did he scoop her up, taking care to support her head against his chest before he carried her back to his car hidden behind a small rock formation.

Hold her, just a little longer. Hold her and enjoy the moment.

Fuck, he was being a bastard. He'd attacked her, knocked her out, and now he wanted to snuggle with her. What the hell was he thinking? "Get your head back in the game, Orion. Before you make a mistake." *Shit, so much for staying silent.*

Take Down

With police-issue zip-tie cuffs and duct tape, he secured Carolyn Grant and wrapped her in a blanket in the back seat, using the seat belts as extra restraint points. He debated adding a blindfold but ruled against it. When she woke she'd be disorientated, but there was no point in adding to her fear. It took a few moments to make sure she would be both safe and secured before he got into the driver's seat, started the engine, and drove to her car. Another five minutes saw Carolyn's car moved off the road, out of immediate line of sight.

"Fucking heels." His shins would feel that for days to come. He glanced at the woman. Not heels in the traditional sense, but good solid shoes, ideal for walking. He grunted, shaking his leg to try to ease some of the pain, but it didn't work. "Cocksucking son of a bitch," he muttered, glaring at his leg. Rubbing it wouldn't help. He'd only feel the tenderness under his fingers, and that would add to his growing bad mood. "Last time I do this. No more snatch and grabs. Especially not women." A woman he wanted to hold, touch, to taste her every inch of skin. He growled and slammed the palms of his hands against the steering wheel.

No going back now. If he untied her, she'd report the incident and then, well, there was a decent chance he'd be arrested for assault and attempted kidnapping.

He pulled out his phone and sent the coded message, waiting only long enough to receive a reply from Michael, one of the men he worked with, before he set the phone down. No texting and driving for Kyle, no sir. Not when something that dumb not only put his ass at risk but the lives of others as well. He'd keep out of reach just in case his pretty little package decided to try to reach out and touch someone.

With one last look at the secured unconscious woman in the back seat, he turned his attention to driving. He had an hour, tops, on the road before he'd reach the ranch house the company had rented. All he had to do was hold her there for a day, two at most, before transport would arrive, and then, well, then get her to her sister, and the woman would be off his hands.

He should have been relieved, so why did the thought sit like a lead weight in the pit of his stomach?

Take Down

Chapter Four

Carolyn's head pounded, and she knew even before ever attempting to open her eyes that it wouldn't improve anytime soon. Pressure pulsed behind her eyes, across her temples, and tightened her throat. She swallowed hard, trying to clear her throat. It didn't help. She frowned. Something shuddered beneath her, vibrating, and it took a moment before she realized she was in something moving. A vehicle? *Car. I'm in a car.* Carolyn listened closely. Not her car though. The sound was wrong for that, and she wasn't in the front seat. No, she was lying down. She scowled, trying to make sense of it all before the fog cleared enough for the pieces—or some of them—to fall into place. Back seat?

Why would she be sleeping in the back seat of a car that obviously wasn't her own? That part didn't make sense. Had something happened? Well, duh, obviously something had. Carolyn was tempted to shake her head, but the pain warned her against such actions. What was she missing here?

Her thoughts remained fogged. A low pounding in the back of her head added to her inability to think straight.

Think. You're not an idiot.

No, but she was a woman with a nasty headache and aching muscles. Carolyn tried to move, but her body wouldn't obey her, not fully. She twisted to the left, but something held her in place, and the idea of falling off the back seat and into the back of the seats in front of her, or worse, into the floor space between front and back, wasn't appealing. Fine, all she had to do was figure out what was holding her in place, and did it affect everything? Her head, she could mostly move that, but doing so only confirmed the presence of her headache when the pounding increased. Being in the back of a vehicle was confirmed when she touched something sticking out from the inside of a door: the armrest and door handle Was she still half asleep? She opened four eyes and blinked, trying to clear her vision, the urge to yawn pulling at her lips. Lips that wouldn't part. Had they stuck together somehow? Her throat was sore; maybe she was ill?

Why would she be asleep in a car? *Stop, breathe, and think.* She struggled to put the pieces together, but her mind remained fogged. When had she last had such trouble waking up? Her head continued to pound even as she attempted to make sense of the situation.

Had she really fallen asleep or—

Memories crashed down on her. Attacked! Fuck, she'd been grabbed and attacked. She hissed, trying to sit up. Something held her in place. Restraints on both her wrists and ankles. There was something across her mouth but nothing over her eyes. He'd left her the ability to see, at least for now.

A man. The feel of his body had returned with the rest of her memories. Strong and yet lean. Taller than herself and damned dangerous. She'd fought, hadn't she?

Yes, she'd kicked, clawed, struggled with everything she had, but it hadn't helped. He'd overpowered her. Everything she'd learned about defending herself had either been forgotten or had failed, but why? The pressure around her throat. Of course. She'd barely had time to fight back before she'd begun that slip into the darkness.

Panic slashed at her. Her heart raced, cold sweat beading down the length of her spine even as her stomach tightened and knotted, threatening to spill its contents. She focused on her breathing; being sick wasn't an option. With her mouth covered, she'd gag, maybe even choke.

Not a victim. I won't let myself die as a victim. Fuckin' bastard, I'll kick him so hard they'll have to perform surgery in order to find his balls!

She swallowed once, twice, and a third time, forcing her rebellious stomach back under control. Not weak. She wasn't weak, wouldn't allow the fear and doubt to kill her ability to think clearly. If panic claimed her, she couldn't effectively fight back, couldn't find

Take Down

a way break free. Only by remaining calm could she find a means to settle the score with whoever was behind this attack.

Who was he? Why had he grabbed her? She was still dressed, and this hadn't been a robbery. She'd have been left in the road if that were the case. No, she'd been the target, not her car, not her personal items.

Sex thing? Had she been taken for that? To be tossed to someone as a toy? Raped? Was this a matter of revenge?

Cold sweat coated her flesh, her stomach knotted, and bile rose, leaving a foul taste in the back of her mouth.

Calm, she had to remain calm and work through the details.

She looked down at her clothing. Nothing had changed; nothing had been left exposed. In fact, it looked like her kidnapper had taken care to pull down her top, which she knew had been shoved up during the struggle. What if she'd been snatched on behalf of someone else, like a man or woman she'd refused to take on as a client? It wasn't unheard of and was one of the many reasons why she didn't see clients at her home but used a rented space and paid for extra security there. As far as she knew, not one of her clients or would-be clients had ever found out where she lived.

Had someone known about the whip she'd ordered? She couldn't imagine that the Whip Master would have shared that information with anyone. Discretion and security were all a part of this lifestyle. At least, it had been for as long as she'd been involved in it.

She frowned and tried to twist onto her side, but the seat belts and restraints made movement near impossible.

She twisted again, but her wrists and ankles were well bound. Just enough room in order to keep the blood flowing, but not enough that she could slip her wrists free.

"Settle down. You're not going to break free anytime soon." A warm, rich voice reached out from the driver's seat, causing her thoughts to stutter. Why hadn't she thought about the driver before now? "You're not the first woman I've bound, and I doubt you'll be the last."

Did she know that voice? Something nudged at the back of her mind, but she couldn't place it. So, she wasn't the first woman he'd seized, or did he mean something else entirely? She swallowed, trying to clear her throat. There'd been a sexual connotation to his words, or was her mind filling in pieces for the sake of sanity? Fuck, she hated not being able to speak.

The helplessness got to her. She wasn't submissive, and this wasn't a game she liked to play. She growled and kicked, struggling to find a way free of the bonds. It was stupid, and she knew it! With a snarl into the gag, she forced herself to stop even as rage shuddered through her helpless form.

"Fighting isn't going to help. We'll be stopping soon enough. If there's a real problem, kick the door, but if you lie to me, try to get me to pull aside without good reason, then I'll tan your backside so hard you'll be sleeping on your stomach for at least a week." Cold steel tinged his words.

Carolyn paled but kept silent this time and not just because of the gag. That voice, she knew it, if she could only remember from where.

"Relax, you've been through a lot. Your throat will be sore, and no doubt you'll have a headache. I'm sorry about that, but it was safer than drugging you. Never know how someone's going to react to a drug." His tone became reasonable, strong but tempting. In other circumstances she might have relaxed, listening to his words, waiting for the next one to tempt her.

No. She couldn't think like that.

Kidnapper. Enemy. Let him think me easily taken. I'll strike when he least expects it.

Would that work now that she'd attempted to fight free? Maybe. It was worth a try. She let her eyes close, forcing her body to relax. Fighting and burning energy that she didn't have to waste when it would do her no good was a fool's mistake.

She listened in an attempt to keep track of the noise beyond

Take Down

the car, though she fought against a pull caused by the vibrations of the engine that would lull her back to sleep. She wasn't tired, but it would have been so easy to let sleep take her. The sounds changed as the journey continued. They'd been on proper roads for some time, but now the noise shifted. A secondary road? Still paved but missing the noise of steady traffic. Here they passed only a few other cars and once a larger vehicle—an eighteen wheeler?

Carolyn opened her eyes, turning her head just enough so she could catch the play of lights. Anything that might help her track where she was would be a bonus.

The car slowed down, and with it came a flicker of lights. Red? She frowned as the pieces fell into place. Traffic lights. A small town or something else? She strained, trying to hear more, but that was a lost cause. Anger bubbled back into life.

No, keep it under control.

Anger and fear both ran the risk of reducing her to a blubbering wreck, something she'd refused to be since leaving her family behind. Her father had been capable of tearing into her emotionally, the look and the harsh words, threats as he'd torn her down time and again after that woman had walked into his life.

Shit, Carolyn barely even remembered what the man was like prior to that. She recalled vague images of something warm and tender, yet she'd known there was something more in him. A father she'd loved, looked up to, reached out to, but the damage had been done. Tears stung her eyes, and she blinked hard and fast.

Don't. Not the time. Not the place.

The car moved, and she continued to listen. The road changed, the sound more a crunch than a rumble of movement over a paved road. Time passed, and she tried to count, though even as she did Carolyn realized it was a waste of time. Minutes passed before the car stopped. A door opened, and the driver stepped out only to return again and repeat the process after driving forward a little more.

Gate?

An old-fashioned gate, maybe a farm or ranch? Though it could equally have been the entrance to a small private road leading up to a house. Either way it no longer mattered. She was lost, and that knowledge added to the knots in her gut.

Carolyn shivered and waited. She silently counted, trying to track the distance—longer than a short driveway but less than a mile? What little information she had added up to a whole lot of nothing. Her hands clenched, nails digging into palms only to release them a few moments later. Hurting herself wouldn't help the situation.

When the car stopped this time, it was different. The engine turned off, and her kidnapper stepped out of the vehicle, coming around to the door closest to her head. The door opened, and she tensed, heart racing though she tried to appear calm. Letting him know she was afraid would give him the upper hand.

Stupid, he has that already. I'm bound, helpless, gagged. What more of an upper hand does he need?

Strong hands reached in under her arms, the grasp firm, unyielding as he pulled her out and shifted her until she was nestled in against his chest. She twisted a little, trying to make out his features and keep herself from leaning against him. The unforgiving darkness of the night and his grip denied her the opportunity to identify her captor or pull back from his chest.

A dozen steps took them up onto a small deck and then in through a door. Light stung her eyes, blinding her afresh until she squinted, giving her vision a moment to adjust, but even as her sight cleared, her captor set her in a chair and turned to look at her.

"Well now, Mistress Lyn. We've got a bit of a wait before transport arrives, so the question is what to do with you until then?" A pair of hazel eyes narrowed, and a dangerous, playful smile touched his full, sensual lips. "Any suggestions?"

Carolyn blinked.

The man from the demo.

* * * *

Take Down

Kyle lifted the silent woman out of the back of the car, holding her against his chest as he kicked the door closed and headed for the ranch-style house. He'd left a couple of lights on before he headed out to collect Carolyn, something he was now grateful for as the ground was uneven in places, and he wasn't entirely sure about the steps that led up onto the deck. Shit, the last thing he needed was to trip and make a complete fool of himself.

Why the hell would I care what she thinks of me? Not like I'm going to have anything to do with her after I deliver the blasted woman to her sister.

Uh-huh, of course. He'd hand her over, walk away, and never speak to or think of her again. Even he was having problems buying that one.

He kept silent until he'd set Carolyn down in the chair and let his gaze trace slowly over her bound form. No matter what he felt, he wasn't going to let his captive know what was going on with him. All she would see, if he had anything to say about it, was a calm, confident professional following through with the task at hand.

"I'm not about to kill you, if that's what you think. You're perfectly safe with me; this is all business."

He offered a smile as he went over his actions. Maybe he should have explained that before letting her see his face? Shit. Had she thought she was going to die so she couldn't identify him? *Fuck, I didn't think that one through. Fine, keep her calm and move on from the mistake.*

"Well now, Mistress Lyn. We've got a bit of a wait ahead of us before transport arrives, so the question is what to do with you until then?" He met her gaze, noting the slight change in her eyes, a widening combined with a flash of anger? His lips quirked at the thought. It didn't matter that he found her attractive; he wouldn't act on it. This was work, and she wasn't a willing submissive waiting for his touch, no matter how he might want it to be otherwise. "Any suggestions?"

He let his gaze move back down to her covered mouth. "Ah, of course. Hard to join in the conversation when there's duct tape in the way."

Kyle chuckled and turned away, reaching for the bottle of baby oil and cotton wool he'd set out before leaving earlier in the day. "Now, don't get any kinky ideas, at least not yet. This is to make sure I don't cause any damage. As I mentioned, you're safe. I'm not going to harm you. That's not what I've been paid to do." Would that statement help or hinder? He dabbed oil onto a large cotton wool ball, soaking it before he began to apply it to the outside of the tape, taking care to rub it into the edges. "It will need to sit for a few minutes before we take this off." *I doubt this is something she's ever had to do.* No, duct tape wasn't in the standard box of tricks for professional Dominants.

Carolyn scowled.

"No point in being angry with me, though I understand why you feel that way. This is just a job." Kyle met her gaze, a small smile touching his lips. Would she have stomped her foot if she'd been free to do so? *Not likely. She's not into childish reactions.* No, this was a woman who would have aimed for his groin, eyes, and throat. He had bruises on his shins and right arm from her self-defense attempt. He glanced down at his arm. Deep scratches marred his flesh, and he'd have to clean them unless he wanted to give infection a chance to set in. "Once I've got that tape off your mouth I'm going to clean up. Then you can scream all you want. All it's going to do is annoy me and waste energy. We're at least a couple of miles away from the nearest house, but the choice is yours. I'll be happy to let you see for yourself, if need be."

If she thinks we're alone she won't waste the energy. She's too smart to make that mistake.

Her eyes narrowed, lines furrowing across her brow.

"Let's see if this is going to work. Let me know if it hurts." He reapplied oil to the cotton wool and reached for the corner of the duct tape. He tugged at the tape, smoothing more oil onto the lifted edge of the tape as he removed it. Carolyn remained silent during the slow, painstaking process, but in his eyes, it was worth it. The last thing he wanted to do was pull off skin along with the tape. "Almost there," he assured her as he worked on the tape. "We'll need to get the residue off, but no harm done."

A low, deep growl vibrated from the back of her throat.

He didn't react to the growl, though the urge to do so threatened to consume him. Carolyn was fire-filled, willing to fight, challenging him with growls. Oh, he'd love to get his hands on this one in a more intimate manner.

His cock pulsed, desire building at her defiance, and he couldn't help but picture her willing and eager in his arms, though he tried to hide his reaction. It was one thing to struggle against a willing woman. Some submissives enjoyed being partially overpowered, but this wasn't a sub coming to him for an evening of fun.

Still, that didn't prevent thoughts flickering through his mind. Her naked, spread eagled on his bed—or any bed—begging for his touch. A touch he would deny her until she screamed the word, *Master*.

Down, boy, he informed his rebellious body. *There'll be willing women at the club when all this is over and done with.*

Kyle pulled the remaining duct tape away from her lips before he rose, stepping away from the woman and the chair, taking the oil and cotton wool with him. A moment later he returned with a warm, soapy washcloth. "This should help with the rest of it. The baby oil will have broken down most of the adhesive." He flashed a smile, meeting her gaze. "You're angry, and you've every right to be, but you're wasting that anger on the wrong person. Just the hired hand here!"

"Hired. Hand." She spat out the words. Her gaze flashed defiance as she lifted her chin, her face a mask of calm that wasn't reflected in her gaze.

"Yup, this is a job. I was hired to bring you in. Nothing more, nothing less." His gaze never left her face. If he was honest with himself, she had every right to be angry with him, even if this was nothing more than a job. It had been his hands on her body, his arm around her throat as he'd carefully applied the sleeper hold, and right now he was the only possible target for her fury. That wasn't, however, going to prevent him from trying to calm her down and get her to turn her anger on the true reason for her capture.

"Who?" A single growled word.

He paused, watching her, waiting for the right moment. When he saw a tightening around her eyes and a slight change to the set of her jaw, only then did he answer, his words cold as for the first time he let his distaste for the assignment slip through. "Your sister. Cassandra Grant."

Take Down

Chapter Five

My sister? Carolyn stared at the man, searching for some sign that he was lying. Was this a joke? No, it couldn't be. He knew who she and her sister both were. "Why?"

"Paperwork." He didn't look away from her.

She blinked. Paperwork? The death of her father or something else? Shit, there was too much going on to be able to dig through the mess without more information. "Explain." *Oh great, he's reduced me to one-word sentences.* She was getting her point across. That was all that mattered.

His powerful shoulders tightened and then he shrugged. "Not my place to explain."

"You're just the hired hand. Got that part." She watched him, gaze narrowing. Hired hand or not, he knew more than he was willing to tell. Microexpressions twitched across his features. Lines appeared and disappeared beneath his eyes. If she'd blinked at the wrong time, she'd have missed it. Something about this job disgusted him. Was it her? "You've met my sister?"

"Briefly." His tone changed, becoming clipped.

How much did Cassandra share with him?

"You dislike the job, but you took it on anyway." She didn't let her gaze move away from his. "Interesting." So, this was all about the money, but tying a woman up was what? Something he enjoyed in his personal life?

His gaze shifted for a second from her face to her body and back again, leaving her skin tightening beneath the caress of his eyes

Carolyn smiled. Yes, tying a woman up for pleasure was something he'd enjoy, but this kidnapping thing wasn't his normal gig. At least not when it came to women. "So, let me get this right. Normally if you're retrieving someone, it's a man and there's the potential for violence involved. Bounty hunting and—let's think." She deliberately let her gaze move over his body, taking in the lean muscle, the power in his body before she met his gaze once more.

"Security."

Her kidnapper cracked a wry smile and sat down in an armchair opposite her. "You expect me to answer that?"

"You just did." If she'd been wrong, the smile would have been different, confident instead of wry. *Thank God for all those lessons from Mistress Michaela.* That woman had been a godsend. From the first, the older Dominant had taken Carolyn under her wing, teaching her the tricks of the trade including how to observe others and translate body language.

He leaned back into the chair. "We'll be leaving for Minnesota as soon as the transport gets here."

Transport. She mulled over the possibilities. Driving would take too long and increase the risk of him being caught. Contract or not, kidnapping was illegal. Trains would offer an even greater chance of arrest. That left only one viable option. "Private plane."

His left eyebrow arched. "You don't miss much."

"I try not to." She shifted on the chair and then raised her bound hands. "Are you going to keep me like this?"

"Not all the time, no. Though I'd be a liar if I didn't admit that you look attractive that way." His eyes half closed.

She had to remain calm. He already had the upper hand. "Do you have a name, or should I just call you asshole?"

He snorted, shaking his head. "Hmm, a name. Well, I suppose that would make life easier." He paused letting his gaze linger on her face. "What would you like it to be?"

Laughing wouldn't help, though the temptation was there. *What would you like it to be indeed!* That was the line you stumbled across all too often with the sub players or rent-a-subs. "Name." Carolyn focused, adding a hint of command to the word. If the man had any submissive tendencies, they'd show through now. "Now, boy."

"Nice try, *Mistress* Lyn." He licked his bottom lip. "But I'm afraid the sub costume was just for show. Still, I can't blame you for try-ing."

Take Down

Well, shit. Still, she hadn't expected it to work. Not with the impact he'd had at the club and his all too obvious, to her at least, dominant presence. It wasn't going to stop her from pushing again. "Well, if you don't give me your name, I'll have to find one that suits you, like...worm."

He flinched.

Got you.

"Perhaps slug would be a better fit." She pretended to give the name serious consideration.

"Let's go with something a little easier on the tongue like..." He paused and then gave a half shrug. "Kyle."

Is that his real name? The shrug and pause suggested not, but there was something about the way he said it. If it wasn't his real name, it was one he'd used before. "Then Kyle it is, for now at least. Worm works as well if you piss me off too much." Carolyn forced her voice to remain calm as her body let her know there were other needs. Ones she'd ignored until now. "Now, untie me. I need to use the restroom."

"No *please*?" He chuckled and rose. "I should make you beg or at least ask politely."

She didn't look away. Weakness, any sign of it, was something he'd use against her. "I don't beg."

"A challenge, and you're tempting me to put to the test."

"But not something you were hired to do, and I doubt my sister would be pleased if I were left to wet myself." She wouldn't blush. It wasn't in her nature, no matter how hard he tried to nudge her into taking the submissive role. "Untie me."

He snarled, rolling his eyes. "Fine, but only because I have no desire to clean up after you. Bloody woman, you'd do it just to be a pain in my ass."

Carolyn smiled, letting her own gaze move down his body, taking in the curve of his muscles, the play of strength beneath his clothing. Yes, she could just imagine being a pain to that sweet and tautly shaped backside. How would he take to a strap-on? A plug first, obviously. This wasn't the type of man who normally let someone top him, but maybe...

"Whatever's going through your mind, forget it." He growled even as he cleared the distance between them. "You'll need to stay still. I don't want to hurt you." He drew a pair of wire cutters from his jeans and moved to her ankles, slicing them free with a practiced ease.

"You've done that a time or two."

"Not my first rodeo."

Carolyn held out her wrists. The wire cutters made short work of the flexi-cuffs, and in a moment she was free to rub her wrists. The movement caught his attention, and he grabbed her hands, turning them so he could look at her wrists even as she tried to pull free of his grasp.

"Damn," he muttered. "You're hurt."

She glanced down at her captured wrists. "It's nothing; they'll heal." Vivid red lines combined with scuffing of the skin marred her pale flesh.

"Shouldn't have happened. I wasn't hired to hurt you." He turned her wrists again, taking care not to twist her arms as he did so. "No bleeding, but it came close in places."

That she wasn't going to argue with. "If I hadn't struggled, it wouldn't have been so bad." No point in lying about that. They both knew any fighting would have added to the abrasions.

"If I'd chosen another means of securing you, it wouldn't have happened at all." He grunted and let go of her wrists. "At least your ankles won't be as bad, but I want you to check them when you go to the bathroom."

"Which would be where?" She flexed her toes within her shoes. Small pulls made her aware of bruising that was, even now, forming around her ankles. He was right. It wouldn't be as bad, but there would still be some small marks she'd have to check.

Kyle stepped back, giving her room to move. "Down the hall." He gestured behind him. "Clean towels, soap, all the usual things. If

Take Down

there are cuts I've missed, let me know. I'll need to look at them."

"You wouldn't trust me with a first-aid kit?" Presuming he had one.

"You, with scissors? No, I like my skin in one piece."

"Ah, yes. I forgot that there might be scissors in a kit." With a low groan she rose, rolling out her shoulders and shifting her weight onto the balls of her feel. She ached, her throat was sore, and with moving, she felt every small bump, scrape, and bruise that now marred her body. *Fuck, I'm going to feel this in the morning.*

"Do you need assistance?"

"No." Her stomach knotted at the thought of his hands on her body, only to release and be replaced by giddy butterflies. *Oh hell no, not going there. Yes, he's cute, handsome, lickable even, but fuck that!*

Lickable? When had that become a part of the equation? She was tired, confused by the attack, and still recovering from the grip he'd locked on her throat. She wasn't sexually interested in the son of a bitch who had snatched her!

Without another word, she walked stiffly away from the chair and down the small hall. The home appeared to be, at least from what she was able to see, a single story ranch-style house. Old, but well cared for, last decorated sometime in the late '70s or early '80s. The door to the bathroom confirmed her beliefs, and a quick check revealed that it lacked a lock.

That didn't surprise her. Why would he allow her access to a room she could lock herself into? No, the man wasn't a fool. Delicious, sensual, and wicked, but not a fool. She growled under her breath. No matter how tempting he might be, he was off limits. *At least until this entire thing is over and done with.*

Carolyn sighed and rubbed her temples. Despite being hired to snatch her, Kyle had been gentle. Even the method of knocking her unconscious, though frightening at the time, had been careful. Sure, a sleeper hold had its risks, but now as she thought it through, he could have chosen far more dangerous methods.

She traced one finger over her lips. The duct tape. A less careful man would have ripped it off her mouth, tearing skin in the process. Yet he'd taken the time to ease it away. Not the actions of a brute but a man doing a job. One he—from how he'd reacted earlier—didn't agree with.

She closed her eyes, going over what she knew.

Kyle was strong, handsome, and a Dominant. In other circumstances she might have spent time with him, a drink, a meal, polite conversation as they grew to know each other.

The thought caught her off guard, and heat rushed across her cheeks.

Why would she want to do that?

He was a Dominant, and she didn't "do" Dominants unless they came to her to explore submission. Yet her body responded to him, heat growing when she thought of him and that sexual ache, that need, those were things she had to ignore when it came to Kyle.

Once Kyle turned her over to Cassandra, they would never see each other again.

Why did that thought disturb her?

Stop thinking about him.

Before he might have a chance to see what was going on, Carolyn stepped into the bathroom and closed the door behind her. Once she'd taken care of the essentials, Carolyn flushed the toilet, rearranged her clothing, and washed her hands in the pale green sink. Only then did she let her attention move to the all-too-small window.

She turned off the light, moved to the sink, and leaned in, resting her hands on the edge, peering out through the glass. Darkness greeted her. She twisted, trying to see to either side. Nothing broke through the night beyond the soft glow that emanated from the house that was, for the time being, her prison. She was, as he had implied, far enough away from humanity to make any chance of escape slim at best.

Well fuck, so much for that idea. Where the hell are we?

Take Down

She couldn't even be certain how long she'd been out cold. Were they on the other side of Vegas? She groaned, lowering her head as she rested on the sink. "This sucks," she mumbled into the otherwise empty room.

The man knew what he was doing, not that there'd been any doubts leading up to this point. If there was a chance to escape, it would involve getting her hands on the keys to his car. She nibbled on the inside of her lip. Not impossible. He was a man. The way he looked at her made it clear he was interested in her on a sexual level, and she wouldn't be the first woman, or man for that matter, who used her body to get what she wanted.

Fine. She could do it.

Be honest. You want to do it.

Chapter Six

Kyle watched as Carolyn walked down the hall and vanished into the bathroom. She was exhausted, but pride and strength kept the woman on her feet, and any new offers of assistance would only sharpen the edge of her temper. Not something he wanted to risk. *Damn, that's one hell of a woman. What would she be like under the hands of the right man, or does she prefer women?* It would be safer for him if she had been a lesbian, but his research suggested bi with an equal interest in both genders. His gaze lingered on the full, firm curves of her ass. Even marked by the dust of the road, that was an ass he wanted to inspect, up close and personal.

Temptation pulled at him, but Kyle resisted the urge to follow the woman and listen at the door of the bathroom. He wasn't that kind of guy, and besides. The bathroom offered no source of escape or help for her. She didn't know where they were, nor did she have a viable means of escape. The car was locked, the keys on his person, and she lacked the tools to break into the vehicle to seek a way out. As for neighbors, it had to be a good ten-mile hike to the nearest house, with the town another five miles beyond.

Taking advantage of the moment, Kyle moved to the front door and checked the locks, including the extra one he'd fitted himself. Without a key, she wouldn't be able to leave. The windows weren't locked, but he'd set alarms on each of them. If she worked out how to open them—which in truth wouldn't be that hard—the squawking alarm would prevent an easy escape. *And if she still runs after triggering an alarm, I'll tan that sweet ass of hers so she can't sit down without feeling the touch of my hand.*

His gaze narrowed as he turned his attention back to the hall. Would she try to find a way out of the small bathroom window? If so, he'd hear the alarm, but the window wouldn't allow for simple escape, and she was smarter than that.

Sounds filtered past the closed door: the flush of a toilet and then the running of water into the sink. She wouldn't stay in the

Take Down

bathroom much longer, perhaps a minute or two, enough to make sure she wouldn't give away what she was thinking. Except he'd already seen glimpses of something, an interest she would deny and—

I'm doing it again.

Yeah, he was. Kyle glanced at his watch. Nearly midnight. Normally he, like nearly everyone else he knew, would have checked his phone, but there was no way in hell he was letting Carolyn near his phone. Even the safety of a pin number wasn't a guarantee. There were ways around that, including using the 911 system. No, that phone was well out of reach, locked away in the center console of his car. The battery had been slipped into the trunk, just in case.

The door opened, and he turned his full attention back to the approaching woman. "Better?"

"Yes." She gave a slight nod.

He let his gaze linger on her face. Smudged purple had formed beneath her eyes. "We're going to call it a night."

"Worn you out already?" A smile twitched at her full, sensual lips.

"Not in the way I'd have preferred," he admitted.

"Ah, but this is a job, so I'm off limits?" Carolyn closed the distance between them but kept just enough of a gap that she was out of immediate reach.

"Yes."

A wicked light danced within her eyes. "Pity."

Careful, she's tired and recovering from the snatch. She doesn't mean it. But what if she did? His cock swelled at the thought, and he inhaled, held it, and then let what he hoped was a calming breath out through parted lips. "We'll be sharing the same room." Not what his original plan had been, and the sane part of his mind protested the moment he'd spoken.

"Hmmmm." She licked her bottom lip and let her gaze deliberately move up and down his body.

"Cut it out, Carolyn." He growled; the muscles down the length of his back tightened. Damn the woman. This was either deliberate and she was playing a game with him, or she really wasn't recovered from the pressure he'd been forced to put on her throat. "I'm tired, you're tired, and neither of us want to make that mistake." *Liar, liar, pants on fire.* Oh God, did he want to make that mistake and then make it again if she was half as good as his imagination suggested.

"Are you sure about that?" She shifted her weight onto the balls of her feet, arching her back a little to lift her full, tempting breasts.

"Very." He deliberately didn't look at those breasts... Well, for the most part. "Do you need something to drink? Water?" *Throat, think about her throat and the potential damage done to the tissues there.*

"Nothing stronger?"

"Water." He struggled against the urge to growl. Damned woman was pushing his buttons.

"Spoilsport." She pushed out one hip, resting a hand on the opposite hip. "You ruin all my fun."

He bit back a groan. No, he wasn't going there. Not this time. Not anytime soon if his common sense had anything to say about the situation. "It's. Late."

Carolyn rolled her eyes. "Fine, yes, water would help. For some odd reason I have a sore throat and a headache. Though I'm sure you could offer something to coat my throat." She slowly and very deliberately traced her gaze down from his chest to his groin and back again.

His cock, her lips, his hand in her hair as he thrust into her mouth, his body tight, hungry and needing release. *No!* This wasn't going to happen. "Keep it up and I'll gag you." Could she see the effect she was having on him? *Yeah, she knows. That's why she's doing it.* "Come with me. We'll get you some water and then try to get some sleep." *Without wet dreams.* Fuck, that would be the last thing he'd need—lying next to her on the bed, albeit a king-size bed, knowing she was within reach as his mind spun infinite erotic images of the wicked woman sleeping next to him.

"A gag. Now would that be an organic one?" Breathy laughter followed the words. "No, I think not. You'd run the risk of finding something bitten off—purely by accident of course."

"An accident would suggest an innocence that doesn't become you." But damn, did he want to feel his cock sliding in and out of her mouth. He growled softly, but led the way into the kitchen. "Cups are over there." He stepped out of the way, letting her gain access to the sink.

"A gentleman would have brought me the water." She flashed a smile over her shoulder before she turned her attention back to the faucet with a black plastic picnic mug in hand.

"I never claimed to be a gentleman." *But damn, I'm going to have to be a bloody saint if I want to keep my hands to myself tonight.*

"I'm beginning to understand that." She turned, leaning her back against the sink as she sipped the water.

For a moment he said nothing, letting her drink in peace until a yawn cracked her features. She was just as tired as he was, which made sense after everything she'd been through. "We need to settle. Sleep will do us both the world of good." Yeah, sleep. That was all he wanted, right?

Carolyn nodded, closing her mouth at the end of the yawn. "Sorry, that kinda crept up on me." The shadow smudges beneath her eyes had increased, the lines across her brow furrowing until she gave her head a quick shake. "Maybe we should call a truce on…on whatever this is until morning?"

"Sounds workable to me." But he didn't buy it for a second. "Down the hall, turn left, and then the first door on the right." There was a second bedroom, and the original plan had been to settle her in there if they'd had to wait for any real length of time, but now the thought of leaving her alone where she might have a chance to figure out a means of escape didn't sit well with him.

No, being honest, he wanted to sleep next to her. To be able to reach out and brush his fingers over her cheek in the middle of the night. Not that he'd take it any further than that. *And just who am I trying to convince? Come on, stop beating this thing to death. I want her, she might actually want me, and all I'm doing is driving myself insane by denying the desire.*

"You expect me to sleep in my clothes?" She glanced back at him before opening the door to the bedroom, the cup of water still in her hand.

"It's that or naked." He shrugged. "Your choice there." *Please don't choose naked. I'm not Superman.*

"Don't you have a spare shirt, T-shirt, vest? Something?" She tugged at her own T-shirt. "If I'm going to have to wear this tomorrow, I'm going to feel, well, gross, if I've also slept in it."

He could understand that. "Yeah, fine, I've got a couple of spare shirts."

She turned and then stopped. "There's only one bed."

"Yes, I thought I made that clear." He had, hadn't he?

"So, where are you going to sleep?" She glared at him.

Hmm, ready to tease but not ready to take it to the next level. Interesting. "In the bed, same as you."

She swallowed. Hard. "I see." She glanced around the room and nodded to the floor. "I can always make up a bed on the floor."

Kyle smiled, his gaze meeting hers. "I don't think so. You'll sleep on the bed. With me. That way if you try to get up or slip out of the house, I'll know about it." No way in hell was he going to let Carolyn slip past him. "There's no point arguing with me, so you might as well save your energy." He nodded toward the bed. "Get yourself settled. I'll wait outside for you to change, but think on this. How you lie down is how you're going to be secured because if you think I'm going to go to sleep without tying you up first, you're out of your ever-loving mind."

Take Down

Chapter Seven

Carolyn scowled and took a step toward Kyle, her voice soft, little more than a whisper. "Tie me up? You really think I'm going to meekly let you tie me up just so you can get a decent night's sleep? Is that it?"

"Yes."

Nuts. That was it. The man was certifiable. "Not going to happen."

"Not open for negotiation." He smirked, pulled a clean T-shirt out of a bag on the floor, tossed it onto the bed before locking the small padlock on the duffel bag. Only then did he walk out the door, shutting it behind him.

Tension knotted across her shoulders and down into her arms until her hands clenched into fists. Nails dug into her palms as she struggled not to scream, grab something to throw, or worse, collapse onto the bed in a fit of tears. Her heart raced, pulse throbbing even as she turned away from the now closed door and swept her gaze around the room. There had to be something here she could use. A freestanding lamp, an ornament, or a piece of wood—though why there would be a piece of wood just lying around in the bedroom in case a kidnap victim needed something to bash her captor over the head with was beyond her. Still, she looked.

Nothing except the duffel bag and the plastic mug clenched in her hand that was still half full of water. Shit, even the mug was useless. Kyle, or whatever his name might be, was too damned smart for his own good. At least with a ceramic mug she'd have held a potential weapon. Smashing the mug over his head might have only dazed Kyle for a moment, but the broken edge would have then provided a useful weapon.

And he'd have overpowered me, tied me up, likely gagged me for good measure, and I'd still be on my way back to Minnesota.

"Fuck," she muttered. At this rate she'd have to accept the situation, return to Minnesota, and deal with whatever paperwork her sister seemed to think she was needed for. At least then Carolyn could skip town and return to Vegas. Unless Cassandra tried to keep her prisoner there. No, that wasn't her. With a groan Carolyn sat down on the edge of the bed and grabbed the T-shirt he'd left for her.

"What type of man locks his duffel bag?" She ran her fingers over the shirt. It was nothing special, soft black cotton, obviously well worn, and picked up from a Walmart or Target, something of that nature. Kyle wasn't a designer-shirt type of man, which she could appreciate. After all, why would a man in his line of work waste money on a more expensive shirt? If he needed button-down shirts for any reason, they'd be just as simple. Like the man himself.

Carolyn yanked off her own top and toed off her shoes. No, that wasn't fair. Kyle wasn't simple. Intelligent, crafty, strong willed, sensual, with a hunter's grace, toned body, and oh-so-kissable lips.

Cut that out.

She glanced back at the door even as she unhooked her bra. The last thing she needed was for Kyle to walk in and see her half naked. Her jaw clenched as her body denied her protest, crinkling her nipples, and her breath hitched. She caught her bottom lip between her teeth, and she held the soft shirt against her breasts, inhaling deeply. Despite the obvious cleanliness, she could still catch a hint of his scent clinging to the fabric.

Her core clenched, heat coating her inner walls as she closed her eyes. A soft touch of spice and natural male musk combined to tease her senses, tempting her to take another breath. Only when she opened her eyes again did Carolyn realize she was holding the shirt to her face and all but burying her nose into it.

"Oh hell no," she snarled and tugged the shirt over her head. No way was she going to turn into one of those weak-willed, follow-the-guy-around-in-order-to-get-laid types. She never had been, never would be. If she was going to take a man, it would be her doing the taking, not lying passively beneath him, thighs spread so he could get his end wet. Still muttering under her breath. she eased out of her pants and socks, folded her clothes, and looked around. The single piece of furniture in the room was a heavy-looking wooden chest of drawers. Dark wood and yes, with small locks for each drawer.

She frowned and walked over, setting her clothing on top of the otherwise clear dresser before she traced her fingers over the first of the drawers. A quick tug confirmed that they were indeed locked. The patina-marked metal held the workings to delicate-looking locks. If she'd had even a hairpin on hand, Carolyn knew she'd have a decent chance of unlocking one of the drawers—which might give her that oh-so-handy weapon to bash the annoying man over the head.

And then what?

She didn't know where she was or how long she'd been unconscious, which restricted her ability to make a safe getaway. Sure, she could hit him and use the car, but a man like that would have taken steps to prevent such a thing. What if she were wrong about where he kept the keys? They could be hidden and not on his person and the car disabled. What if she hit him too hard and killed him? Or at least seriously hurt him? That would be a hell of waste and— And the bastard had kidnapped her! Okay, not exactly a kidnap, more of a retrieval, at least as far as he was obviously concerned. As angry as she was with Kyle, it was Cassandra she really needed to be upset with. Cassandra was behind all of this. Couldn't she have sent a message with Kyle? Here sister should have given her the chance to make a sane choice to either return to Cassandra or refuse and then Carolyn could continue on with her own life.

"Like I'd ever return, no matter what she said. She had a chance to leave with me. She made her damned choice. Why the fuck can't she respect mine?" Therein lay the real problem. Betrayal. Sisters, especially twins, were supposed to stick together. Weren't they?

Irritated, she tugged the hair tie from the end of her braid and finger-combed it through. She needed a brush or a comb but wasn't about to ask for one. Not as if she needed to look good for anyone, but that wasn't why she normally took care of her appearance. This was about her, about how she felt, not trying to attract his attention— which she already had in spades. With a grunt, she worked out a knot from the long purple waves.

"Ready?" Kyle called out from behind the still-closed door. "Better be. I'm coming in regardless."

Cassandra tensed, turning as the door opened.

Kyle whistled. "Nice."

Confidence warred with uncertainty. Cassandra rested a hand on her left hip, shifted her weight to cock the hip out, and tipped her head to the left, letting a slow, sensual smile claim her lips. "Like what you see?"

"Well, let's see. I'm straight and—" He made a show of pressing two fingers to his neck. "—yup, still have a pulse."

"Sure about that?" Carolyn took a step toward him, deliberately adding a deep sway to her hips. *Come on, Kyle, watch the body. Don't think about what I'm going to do.* If she could distract him and get the small key ring she could see in his jeans, she had a chance here.

"Very, but it's time to cut it out. We need to sleep, and I'm not in the mood for games."

The outline of his cock drew her attention, thick, heavy despite the covering of denim. He could deny it all he wanted, but he desired her. "Pity, I get a lot of men coming to me wanting to explore at least some form of bisexuality. A plug, dildo, pegging, sometimes they even want me to set up a scene where they are *forced* to suck off another guy." There was, of course, no force involved, but the fantasy of it appealed to many of her clients.

"Not my scene." He shrugged. "Lay down." He nodded toward the bed.

"Make me." The words slipped past her lips before her common sense had a chance to kick in.

"It won't end well for you."

"Oh?" She arched an eyebrow.

Take Down

"You wouldn't be the first woman I've spanked, and I won't make it pleasant."

Liquid hunger coated her inner walls, though she faked a yawn. "You're assuming that you'd win." She forced a nonchalance into her shrug that she didn't feel before she wandered to the bed and settled onto her right hand side, battering the pillow for a minute before she gave up and closed her eyes. A hand closed on her ankle, followed by something cold that locked into place. She growled and sat up, glaring at Kyle.

"I warned you about this." With a second click, the prison-style manacle with its long length of chain locked around the bottom of the bed, under the mattress. A scrape of metal confirmed that it had been attached to the frame. "Now, get some sleep. We both need it."

Chapter Eight

Damn the woman. Why was she deliberately trying to make his life a misery? It wasn't going to help her in the long term, and her fight wasn't with him. *Serves me right for taking on the job in the first place.*

Kyle stripped out of his shirt, shoes, and socks, leaving his jeans in place before he lay down on the bed next to Carolyn. The manacles would hold her. Short of having a key or something to pick the lock, she wouldn't be able to slip free in the middle of the night. Sure, they weren't full prison or cop standard, and if she was able to take a good look at them, she'd realize that, but she'd still need something to spring the lock if she wanted to escape. Thankfully her lack of clothing made it clear that she didn't have anything on hand that she could use.

He shoved at the pillow, trying to force it into a form that would offer real support.

The woman didn't move. In fact, if the soft sounds coming from her were anything to go by, she was already asleep. He glanced over. She remained still, except for breathing. Her hair, now loose from the braid she'd kept it in until this point, spread out over the pillow. Her hair was even longer now that it had been released and brushed her shoulders in dark purple waves.

His fingers itched with the need to reach out and run his fingers through those dyed locks. He bit back a sigh. When it came to Carolyn, there was no touching allowed.

Kyle shifted and lay down on his back, his left hand not quite within reach of her sweetly curved ass. It wouldn't have taken much to reach out and cup it, or better yet, roll onto his side and pull the sleeping woman against his chest, pinning her with arm and leg alike. His cock thickened at the thought. This sucked. By the time he turned Carolyn over to her sister, he'd be suffering from a serious case of blue balls.

Would he be able to find a willing woman? That normally

Take Down

wasn't an issue. Both he and several of his friends enjoyed a couple of the local clubs as well as private groups where submissive and dominant women could be found. Hell, he'd played with switches on occasion as well, but when it came to sex, he preferred something more. Sure, he had a few friends with benefits, but despite the common idea that men could separate sex from emotion, he wasn't one of that number. Sex without a connection was just masturbation with another warm body.

It was something Michael had teased him about more times than Kyle wanted to think about.

He yawned. He had to try to get some sleep. Their plane would be here, if everything worked out, by late morning or more likely early afternoon, and when Carolyn regained her strength, she'd give him a run for his money, of that he had no doubt.

Shit, he welcomed the challenge.

* * * *

"You want me," she purred against his lips, sharp nails scraping a path down his back, teasing at exposed flesh. "Admit it. Submit to me, and I'll be yours. I'll take you so high that you'll never want to come back down."

Kyle growled, tugging at the bonds that held him in place. When had he agreed to be bound? This wasn't like him. He wasn't submissive and never bottomed to someone, no matter how tempting they might be. "You know I do, but not like this. Never like this."

"You wouldn't be like this if you didn't want it." She nipped at his bottom lip. "And this." She reached down and wrapped her fingers around his cock. His very naked cock. It throbbed under her fingers, aching for something more than a simple hold. "Well, let's be honest. He wants this."

Kyle growled, struggling once more. Cuffs held him in place against the St. Andrew's cross, locked at wrist and ankles. "Let me go."

"Beg for it." She tightened her hold around his cock. "That's all you have to do. Beg for it and I'll let you go."

Would she? For a moment he was tempted to try, but he wasn't a submissive, and begging—it had never been something that turned him on. Yet he couldn't deny the way his body ached for her.

She released her grip on him and stepped back. A black leather bustier covered her breasts, offering plump curves that threatened to spill out from the confines of the top. Skin-tight pants of the same color painted her legs, leaving a gap between top and pants, exposing her naval. God, how he wanted to taste her there, dip his tongue in and sweep up to her breasts or down between her thighs. He swallowed hard, trying to fight the need within, only to groan as she moved one slender finger to her throat, circling a spot just beneath her chin, an area he knew many women enjoyed being kissed, licked, and nibbled.

"Let me taste you," he pleaded.

"All you have to do is beg properly. You know how to do that, what words are expected." Her finger traced a slow path down her throat to the curve of her breast, following the outline of her raven tattoo. "Say it, beg me, and I'll let you down from there. I might even let you kiss me."

"Only a kiss?" He growled.

"Well, you haven't earned anything more than that." She licked over her bottom lip, leaving it plump and glistening. "What would you do in order to gain something more than a kiss from me, my pet?"

"I'm no one's pet!" He yanked on the bonds, anger spurring him on.

Carolyn laughed.

Wait a minute. This is my dream. Why am I the one tied up? "I'm not submissive."

"Prove it," she taunted and tugged on the strings at the front of her bustier.

Kyle looked away from her, not wanting to see the living, breathing temptation of a woman in front of him. He didn't belong tied up; she did. He scowled, looking at the restraint that bound his left wrist. That didn't belong there. The cross shouldn't exist and…

"Well done." Her soft voice drew his attention. No mocking tones this time or demands that he beg.

He blinked. The St. Andrews cross and restraints were gone. Instead he stood, still naked, looking at Carolyn as she sat on the edge of a bed. His bed. The full king from his house. No dungeon this time, but his bedroom complete with the heavy wooden chest that sat at the foot of his bed. The chest he used to keep his toys out of the way.

His attention returned to the woman on the edge of his bed. Still in her leather bustier, but the pants were gone, a simple black G-string in its place.

"You know what to do, Kyle, but I won't just lie there for you. If you want me, you're going to have to earn me." She rose, tipping her chin, a playfully defiant smile curving her lips. "I'm not submissive. You know that."

"Yes, I do." He stalked toward her. "But in the bed there can be only one alpha."

"One…at a time, that is. Perhaps this time it will be you; perhaps next it will be me…"

"It will be me, each and every time." He reached for her and—

His hands closed on empty air even as his cock punched at the inside of his jeans. Kyle blinked, trying to make sense of what had happened before he turned on his side. She was still dressed in his T-shirt and panties, and Carolyn Grant lay peacefully asleep within arm's reach on the bed.

A blasted dream. One that had betrayed him by kicking him awake before he'd finally tasted the damned woman. What the hell was wrong with him when even his dreams wouldn't offer him the taste he wanted?

And now he had the hard-on from hell.

He rolled off the bed, checking back on the sleeping woman before he snatched up his duffel bag, moved to the door, and eased out of the room. An ice-cold shower was his only hope at this point in time. Perhaps he should be grateful. At least he hadn't woken up with the inside of his jeans coated with his cum. He could only imagine what Carolyn would say about that if his body had betrayed him.

He glanced at his watch. Seven-thirty. He stared at the numbers and shook his head. He'd been asleep for almost six hours, so why did he feel as though he'd barely laid his head on the pillow before being woken by the dream?

Yeah, he needed that shower before he did something stupid.

Take Down

Chapter Nine

The bed creaked beneath her, but Carolyn kept her eyes shut, refusing to allow her muscles to tense. He couldn't know she was awake, not yet at least. He didn't speak as he walked through the room. Kyle didn't approach the bed in his travels but paused long enough to leave her wondering if he would say something before he exited and closed the door quietly behind him. She kept still and began to count under her breath. Only when she reached a count of one hundred did Carolyn open her eyes.

Soft spears of light pierced their way through the curtains, giving a hint to the time of day, but without her phone she couldn't narrow it down to more than sometime in the morning. Maybe early morning? She sat up and looked down at the manacle still locked around her ankle. *He could have unlocked it. How the hell am I supposed to make it to the bathroom with that damned thing still in place?*

She reached out and touched the restraint, following the curve of the metal around her ankle. Simple enough device, but without a means to pick the lock, she would remain chained to the bed. Her jaw clenched. That wasn't going to happen. With a quick glance at the door, her ears straining to pick up any sound that might alert her to his return, she shifted, curling her leg until she could reach under to where the other end of the chain had been attached to the bedframe.

Her fingers brushed against cold metal, coiled springs attached to a simple frame. Not quite what she would have expected when she'd first walked into the room, but it offered possibilities. *Bastard, why couldn't he have taken the easy route in securing me to the bed?* Something like a rope that she could have slipped free from? Easy? Like hell, he'd known exactly what he was doing.

She froze. A low creak, not enough to be a footstep in the hallway, and it had come from the wrong direction. She let out a breath she hadn't even been aware of holding. The sound had come from outside, a tree or something similar. Carolyn reached under the bed, searching for anything she could use. Something caught beneath a nail and she frowned. Barely within reach, the small piece of metal caught again, this time against her forefinger, scraping against her skin.

Was it loose?

She twisted, stretching for it, closing finger and thumb around it. She tugged, losing it for a moment before she reached again and snagged it. It moved with her touch, closer this time. Whatever it was, it had shifted. She focused, catching hold of the metal.

Just a little more.

She tugged, once, twice, three times, and hissed under her breath as something sliced through the pad of her index finger. Carolyn grinned as she lifted the piece of metal wire from beneath the bed. Carolyn watched the door and sat up, sucking her finger to take the sting out of it before inspecting the cut. Small, annoying, and it would bleed for a time, but it would heal. She sucked on it again, cleaning it as best she could, and then turned her attention to the manacle. The wire was a little thicker than she would like, but it would work. She would make it work.

Carolyn shifted on the bed, turning the manacle until she could get to the lock, and probed it with the end of the wire. Her bottom lip caught between her teeth as she pulled it back and tweaked the end before trying again. Time lost meaning. Her entire focus was on the lock.

The lock clicked, the sound so soft and subtle that she almost missed it. With a swallowed cry of joy, she yanked the manacle free from her ankle. One step out of the way, only a couple more to go. She moved from the bed, grabbed her jeans, and pulled them on, stuffing her socks into her pockets before she slipped her feet into shoes. The T-shirt was next, bra, and she tugged on her shirt on before she moved to the chest of drawers.

There had to be something she could use within the drawers. Money, a pair of scissors, information that might reveal where she was. It wouldn't be easy to escape. A man like Kyle wasn't foolish enough to leave the car keys or a cell phone in easy reach, and dashing out into the unknown was more likely to result in her being recaptured or injured.

No, better to find out what she could, locate a weapon if possible, and then make her escape.

She picked the first lock with ease. They were old and simple to negotiate. A tug opened the first drawer but revealed nothing of use. The second drawer, which took a moment longer as the lock was stiff, was another matter entirely. Toward the back of the drawer, hidden beneath old pillowcases was a pocket knife in a simple leather sheath. No fancy corkscrew or bottle opener, no Swiss army knife, a simple knife left behind by some unknown boy.

Carolyn checked the blade but didn't make the rookie mistake of running her finger along the edge. She already had one bleeding finger. She didn't need another. While not razor sharp, the knife would serve well enough should she need it. With a nod, she slid it back into the sheath before stuffing it into her pocket along with the wire she'd used to pick the locks. Hiding the knife meant he wouldn't see it or immediately assume she was armed if he discovered she was free from the manacles before she made good her escape.

With the drawers closed she set her shoulders and—

A soft creak was all the warning she had, barely enough to turn toward the door.

Dark eyes, jaw set, his hair damp and chest glistening, Kyle stood in the doorway. "What the hell?"

Carolyn formed a mask of confidence even as her guts knotted. "Well, did you really think that silly little chain would hold me? Seriously, Kyle, is that the best you can do?"

KYLE'S GAZE FIXED on his prisoner. "The best... Damn, woman, you've got some nerve. If you're trying to push me into making a rookie mistake, it's not going to work." How in hell's name had she released herself from the manacle set? Had she somehow hidden a hair pin or a piece of wire in her panties, her hair, or somewhere else equally ridiculous? All right, so the hair part wasn't so ridiculous, but there'd been nothing there. She'd worn it in a simple braid and then taken it out before settling into bed. Even now it fell in purple waves around her shoulders and down her back, caressing her cheeks with dark waves that tempted his fingers.

Carolyn smiled. "If you insist on keeping a girl restrained, you have to expect her to take steps to escape. After all, you didn't exactly leave me a bathroom option, did you?"

Bathroom? This was about her need to use the damned bathroom? "Uh-huh, fine, right. You know where it is." He stepped to one side and waved at the door. "And then you're going to return to that bed."

She arched an eyebrow.

Fine, so there'd be a discussion about that. He could deal with it once she returned from the bathroom. "Go, now. Before I change my mind."

Defiance flickered across her features, but this time at least she didn't say anything. Instead she sauntered across the room and through the door. He didn't let her out of his sight and turned to follow her down the hall until she vanished into the bathroom. Regardless of what she'd used to pick the lock on her ankle, the window in the bathroom was still too small for her to get through without creating a lot of noise, and then there were the alarms he'd fixed to each window in the house. He could still allow her a moment of privacy as he leaned against the wall.

Besides, watching a woman relieve herself wasn't a kink he enjoyed. That implied a TPE relationship or a means of stripping a submissive of barriers, what some Dominants called a break. Breaking down the walls, stripping them away to that point was something you needed time to do and time to deal with any fallout after the event. How would she take to a break?

He shook himself and focused on the closed door ten paces away. Close enough that he could grab her if she made a mad dash for it, but far enough away to give her the pretense of privacy.

After that trick with the cuffs, does she deserve privacy?

He straightened at the sound of running water, rolling out his shoulders. They needed to talk. This situation didn't have to be difficult. He was doing a job, didn't want to hurt her, and she would be—he presumed—free to leave Minnesota once the paperwork was taken care of. The boss, Harvey Brent, had run a full background check on Cassandra Grant and her family. If there had been even the slightest hint that returning Carolyn to the *loving* arms of her family would result in long-term problems, Brent would have refused the job. Shit, Kyle's boss was careful when it came to taking on clients, and it was extremely rare for them to take on a job that included returning an unwilling adult unless they were wanted criminals. At least it was rare within the confines of the US. Outside of the country such retrievals were easier but still far from an everyday occurrence. That was one of the things that kept the team strong. All seven of them, five men and two women, had repeatedly turned down offers to work for other companies in order to stay with the man they knew they could trust.

The door opened.

"Thought I'd find you there."

Kyle shrugged. "After your little trick with the cuff, where else would I be?"

"You might have found a nice dark hole to crawl in, as befits a worm." Her tone shifted into the cold, crisp voice of a professional Dominant.

"Thought you'd agreed to call me Kyle." *Don't jump. She wants me to react.* Did she have an escape plan in mind? It was possible. "Back in the bedroom."

"I don't think so." She turned, deliberately slowly, and took a step toward the kitchen. "Don't know about you, but I'm hungry."

He moved. Without warning he locked one hand around her left shoulder. "Bedroom."

Carolyn dropped her shoulder and her weight partially down on the left-hand side, using both hands to grab his wrist as she pushed her hip back into him, using the grip, his height and weight against him to roll him over her shoulder. Before he had chance to fight back, Kyle found himself flat on his back in front of her as she took a step back. "I didn't give you permission to touch me."

It's on. He growled, the sound low and dangerous even to his own ears. He rolled onto his stomach and pushed to his feet, keeping a close eye on Carolyn. He was vulnerable on the floor, not something he enjoyed. "Nice move."

"I'd be a shitty Dominant if I didn't know how to defend myself." She took another step back, giving herself just enough room to allow for a warning if he moved against her.

Smart woman. "Fair point, but don't try it again. I'm far more experienced than you."

"Are you sure about that?" A mocking smile claimed her lips. "I'd have thought a man who was experienced would have known better than to pull a dumbass stunt like that one." She let an assessing gaze move over him, lingering on his groin—his cock gave an obliging twitch—before she looked away.

"Dumb..." He wanted to protest, but the truth of it was, he knew better. "Yeah, fine. I underestimated you. It won't happen again."

"Yes, you did, and yes, you will." She pushed a length of purple hair back from her face. "You see an overweight woman—yeah, I know I'm fat—who has to be, what? Ten inches shorter than you? Hm, yeah about that. One who struts across a stage as a Dominant, with willing, panting men ready to do whatever she says, as long as it fits their fantasy, and of course you're going to underestimate her."

Overweight?

He didn't think, he edged, closing in on her. Carolyn's eyes widened in the moment before he crowded her, using that extra height and build to reduce her ability to move. This time he used both hands, grabbing her by one upper arm and the other on her shoulder, closing his grip just enough to press against a nerve cluster. He shifted to the left, making it harder for her to bring up a knee even as he slammed her against the wall, rattling frames and doors alike.

He bared his teeth in a frustration filled snarl, putting his lips only an inch away from hers. "Don't you ever call yourself that again in my hearing."

"W-what?" She blinked, her eyes wide, back arched, full breasts pressed against his chest, nipples hard enough to feel through the shirts they both wore. "I…"

"You. Are. Not. Fat."

She swallowed. Hard. Her pulse pounded beneath his fingers, mouth open as she ran the tip of her tongue over her plump bottom lip. Her breath hitched, thighs parting a little more even as her hips lifted and tilted toward him. "Why would you care what I called myself? Not like I mean anything to you beyond a paycheck, right?"

The words should have forced him to back off. Should have kicked his common sense into action, but they didn't. If his common sense had any objections, it had wandered off, no doubt to spend time in a bar, with a tall cold one and some long forgotten friends—such as restraint. Instead, desire took over.

He closed the small gap between them, lips claiming hers, his tongue sliding into her mouth, finding her tongue as she groaned beneath the assault. He didn't let go, didn't give her a chance to escape. All he knew in that moment was the temptation of her body, her mouth, the play of their tongues as he claimed her mouth as a personal playground. He stroked, explored, stealing her breath until she whimpered, twisting softly between Kyle and the wall. Even then he let up only enough to allow her a chance to inhale before he took what was his once more.

Mine.

This woman had tormented him from the moment she'd walked onto the stage. Her power, strength, and sensuality had called to him. This was wrong; he knew it. He was blowing his career. When Brent found out what Kyle had done, his ass would hit the road so fast he wouldn't have a chance to explain, but in this moment, with Carolyn pinned against the wall, her tongue matching each and every thrust, he didn't care what Brent would do. She was his and she wanted this, needed this as much as he did if her reactions where anything to go by. He knew it was wrong because it went against everything he'd ever held true, yet in this moment he didn't care. You never, ever mixed business with pleasure, never pushed a woman into something she didn't want, and sure as hell didn't make a move on a woman you'd kidnapped and were returning to her family against her will.

He broke the kiss, searching her face for any sign that he'd stepped over the line, when it hit him—at exactly the same time that he felt the touch of the knife against his throat.

He'd just underestimated her and made that damned rookie mistake—again. If that wasn't bad enough, her next words turned his world upside down.

"If you can take this from me, if you can show me that you're the man I believe you to be, then I'll give you what you want. This once, and this once alone, I'll be the submissive willing woman you want in your bed."

Take Down

Chapter Ten

Despite the knife in her hand, he pressed forward, claiming her lips in a fresh kiss.

God, he felt good. Her lips parted beneath his onslaught, her body heating to his touch as she arched under him. The kiss. She should have told him no, pushed him away, fought and struggled, but the sane, sensible part of her mind had hung a DO NOT DISTURB sign on the door and was now merrily opening a bottle of chilled Moscato d'Asti in celebration. *Damned traitorous bitch*. As soon as she was out of this mess, she was going to hunt that part down and give it the spanking it deserved.

Can't do this, shouldn't do this, but damn, I don't want it to stop.

Her nipples hardened, crinkling beneath her bra, and her breasts tightened. Heat stroked sensual fingers up and down the length of her spine before they curved over her hips and past the waistband of her pants. She groaned, hips rolling, tipping toward him, seeking to be closer, to meld their bodies into one. Their tongues fought, stroked and teased, building the fire within her body until her core rippled, clit ached, and the delicious warmth left her panties damp.

He moved against her. The outline of his erect cock made it clear that he was as into this as she was, but one of them had to step back, had to put an end to this before it was too late.

Pulling the blade on him was a dangerous move, but she'd done it regardless. Now, despite the blade still in her hand, she couldn't stop kissing him, didn't want to stop. Too many clothes. That was the problem: they were both wearing too much. Maybe if they… No, she had to stop, think, and regain control.

Sweat beaded across her brow, but she didn't know if it was from fear or desire as she lifted the blade, pressing the tip beneath his chin again as he broke the kiss, the challenge spilling from her lips before she had the chance to rein it in. "Are you sure you want to do this?" He arched an eyebrow, heat dancing in his gaze.

"Yes." A band tightened around her heart. *God, I didn't say that, couldn't have said that. Shit, now what?* She wasn't submissive. It wasn't within her nature. She knew that, had proven that time and again, so why in hell's name had she just made that offer?

"Don't tempt me, Carolyn." He didn't flinch from the blade she still held against his throat. "You throw a challenge like that at a man like me, and you're liable to end up regretting it."

Regret? No, whatever happened, there'd be no regret involved. One of them would end up on the bottom this day, and it wouldn't be her. "And if you lose, if you're unable to take me down, then you'll be the one who kneels, who submits to me."

He swallowed, his pulse racing beneath his chin.

Would he back down now that his own ass was on the line? "Well, what's it to be?"

"Agreed, but not here. Cramped and far too easy to hurt each other, which isn't something either of us have in mind, is it?" His gaze locked with hers. "The bedroom has enough space for this without damaging the room or furniture."

Furniture, space—what else was he going to worry about? Still, she couldn't be angry with the man, not when he was trying to make sure that she wouldn't be hurt in the process. "I have your word that you won't try to disarm me until we are both ready?" Why was she doing this? Had she lost all claim to sense? A take-down scene with a man she knew, without a doubt, wanted to strip her bare, part her thighs, and claim her body completely? *What about my heart and soul? Does he want those as well?*

No, he had no interest in anything more than a shared hour or two of passion. Hot, sweaty sex that would leave them both sated before they parted company and she returned to Minnesota.

What if I want something more?

Stupid. She didn't know him, couldn't ever know him, but they could enjoy this regardless of who won. They could relax and enjoy what was to come.

"You have my word. I won't try to take the knife from you until we agree to begin." He nodded, the move a small one. Understand-

Take Down

able considering that the blade still touched his skin.

With a smile she stepped away, lifting the edge away from his throat before lowering it. "You're going to do well as a submissive, if only this once, Kyle. I'll be sure to put you through your paces." Could she do it? Did she have a chance of winning in a takedown? God, she'd only see such a scene a handful of times in her life, and then it had been a submissive female against a Dominant male. Each time the woman had wanted to lose, though she had fought, struggled, scratched and bitten, much to the amusement of the audience.

Yet the scene had been powerful. Something that had been seared into Carolyn's mind. She, like many, had squirmed—though she'd kept it better hidden than others—as she'd watched the takedown scene unfold. Now, as she walked back with him to the bedroom, fear and desire rippled through her, sending shivers of heated hunger deep into her belly. This was a man she might enjoy submitting to— No, bottoming to. There'd be no true submission. She knew that. He knew that. Yet it might be enough.

It would have to be enough.

A TAKEDOWN SCENE. Of all the things he might have expected, this hadn't been one of them. Not offered from her own lips, at least. His cock thickened, tight and full beneath his jeans at the thought of pinning her down. She would fight, of course, and she had managed to get the upper hand twice all ready, but that would backfire now. She didn't know how often he'd been called to use his skills in a fight. That little knife she held—it wasn't much of a weapon, but it could still be used to cause him serious injury or even kill him. His focus had to be on removing it from her grasp as soon as possible.

She didn't want to hurt him, and he knew how to disarm a man who knew how to fight. Her skills wouldn't be enough to—

Don't underestimate her, not again.

Carolyn led the way into the bedroom, and he closed the door behind them. Spacious with only the bed and chest of drawers in the room. Even his duffel bag no longer offered a trip hazard, as that was still in the bathroom, safely locked away. He'd have to check the bag once this business was done with. If she'd found her way into it, then there were several things she may have stolen, but where would she had hidden them?

Come to think of it, where had she found the knife?

Too many questions and no answers to be had unless he forced them from her. Or she offered them. Not something she was likely to do anytime soon.

Carolyn turned to look at him, her face a mask of calm save for the gleam dancing within her eyes. "So, here?"

"It would seem to be the best option." He watched her, waiting for an answer. "Unless you've changed your mind."

"No, though I wondered if you had." She ran the tip of her tongue over her bottom lip. "You don't strike me as the type of man who has ever bottomed to another before."

"Still convinced that you're going to win, is that it?" He grinned and took a step forward. "Shoes, we should both be barefooted, don't you agree?" That was the norm when it came to a takedown scene.

"Convinced, no, but if I were a betting woman, I know who I'd pick." Doubt flickered across Carolyn's features before she toed off her shoes, revealing bare feet. "As for you, well, let's just say the odds are stacked against you."

He didn't snap a witty comeback at her but instead moved to the left, assessing the space they had at hand. How best to do this? The takedown scenes he'd witnessed varied from simply disarming the submissive to binding them with their hands behind their back and putting the blade or other weapon to the throat of the *conquered* party. He smiled at the thought. They were—in all honesty—barbaric scenes. The warrior capturing and subduing his prize before taking what was his by right of battle, and she fit the idea of a warrior woman, submitting to the stronger party, yet still dangerous if he turned his back on her.

Take Down

No, he didn't need to bind her, but the ideal appealed to him, and he fingered his belt.

"Shall we?" He gestured to the room, his back to the door, blocking it as a potential exit. The idea hit him and he flashed a grin. "If you can get past me and escape this room—with or without the dagger—then I'll concede defeat." He offered the addition to the original agreement. "Otherwise there'll be no true end to this."

"Agreed." She slipped the knife from her pocket, letting the leather sheath hit the floor. She shifted her weight, turning her hips toward him in silent invitation.

His groin tightened, and he forced himself to focus his attention on her hands. The knife gave her a small advantage and was the first thing he'd take care of. "Ready?"

"Ready," she agreed.

Neither of them moved. For several long seconds Kyle watched her, waiting for a sign that she was about to shift. Most would have made a dash for the door, but she was watching him, assessing his plans.

Smart.

Knife fights were normally over very quickly, but this wasn't a standard knife fight. He flexed his fingers, shifting his weight to the left. She responded, tensing before she edged back, varying her stance, her own weight never settling fully on one foot or the other, taking small steps as she watched him Was she about to make a break for it?

Carolyn darted to the right, moving so quickly he barely had chance to adjust his plans. He growled under his breath as he half turned, reaching out to try to wrap his arm around her waist. She twisted at the first touch, shifting her weight onto one foot in a half spin, half kick that lacked true force but still caught him behind his knee.

He stumbled, regaining his balance as he turned and caught her by the hair and winced at her cry. He tugged, using the grip to tip her off balance and back against his chest even as he wrapped his free hand around her throat, applying just enough pressure to let her know she was held. She kicked, snarled, and clawed, but this time she had the knife in hand. He smacked at the hand, slapping the wrist. It didn't work. She still held the blade.

Damnit, if I don't get that out of her hand, she's going to use it.

Carolyn brought the blade back, hesitating before she slashed at his arm, opening up a line of red that was barely more than a scratch. *She doesn't want to hurt me.* Something he was grateful for, but the cut still burned. He had to disarm her before Carolyn managed to do more than scratch him. He arched, just enough to half lift her feet from the floor, but she fought back, slamming heels against his legs and then kicked back and up, barely missing his groin with one heel. Kyle flinched, his balls threatening to crawl their way up into his body.

"Not going to give up," she growled and slammed her heel back again.

He shifted his hips, barely blocking the blow. "Vicious!"

"With good reason!" She tried again, this time slamming her heel back against his thigh.

Kyle turned, carrying her with him as he marched toward the bed. She kicked, twisting as she struggled against him, his body hyperaware of hers as they fought. With a low cry she brought the knife up again, reversing it so the blade pointed backward, only to hesitate again. If this had been a real fight, she'd have struck. Wouldn't have paused, and the knife would have been buried in his body.

With his free hand he slapped out again. The knife had to go.

This time, when he connected with her wrist, she cried out, her fingers loosening their hold. The knife fell, clattering as it hit the floor even as he slammed her onto the bed face first, attempting to use his weight to pin her in place.

"No!" Panic flared through her, carried by the single word.

He paused, holding her against the bed as he released his grip on her throat. Was he doing the right thing? Rape wasn't some-

Take Down

thing he did, and they'd agreed to this, but had she changed her mind? Not the time to ask. Yet he knew, without a doubt, that if she really wanted him to stop, if she changed her mind, he'd back off.

She twisted, her bottom pressing against his groin, her hips lifting in an unconscious reaction before she continued to fight, to kick at him even as she clawed at the bedding, seeking purchase.

"Give up." He leaned in, nibbling the back of her neck.

A tremor ran through her body, and she paused for a breath before she slammed her head back at him. "No!"

He yanked back just enough to avoid the full force of the blow. "You've lost. It's time to give up."

"Never!" Her hands fisted in the bedding.

There was nothing she could do; she was just too damned stubborn to realize that. Using his weight to keep her pinned to the bed, Kyle reached down to his belt, unbuckled it, and slid the leather from the confines of the denim loops. Whatever happened after this, Carolyn had to accept that she had lost. With the belt in his left hand he reached for her right wrist with his free hand, capturing it with ease. She tensed beneath him, faltering for a moment before her fight began anew.

Why in hell's name won't she just give up?

Why would she? This was a woman who needed to know that she had fought every step of the way. That there was nothing she could look back on and chastise herself about at a later date. Without wasting further words, he brought her hand behind her back and looped one end of the belt around it, cinching it tight before he shifted his grip and tried for her left wrist.

She snarled, bringing her hand beneath her, holding it out of reach.

He should have expected that, yet it still came as a surprise, and he swore, struggling to hold the squirming form in place. His cock ached behind the confines of his jeans, and Kyle shifted, unable to deny his desire to be free of the tough confines of the denim. It would have been so easy to yank her pants down and take her like this, but that wasn't what they had agreed on, what she had consented to, and he fought against the urge to slide deep into her wet heat. With his full weight pinning her down, he reached for her arm again, struggling to pull it free, but Carolyn continued to fight him.

"Give. Me. Your. Wrist." He snarled against her ear. "Now!"

Carolyn Grant, Mistress, and all-around stubborn woman shuddered beneath him. For several long moments neither of them moved save for labored breathing. Then, without a word, she eased her wrist out from beneath her body, offering it to him.

It was done.

Take Down

Chapter Eleven

What have I done?

Carolyn turned her head, her gaze moving to her wrist, now trapped in Kyle's large hand. Silently he moved it behind her back, binding it with his belt before either of them spoke again.

"It's over." The words, so simple and softly spoken, punched through her, shattering a wall she hadn't ever acknowledged.

She swallowed, aware of every inch of her body from her bare feet to her nipples now hard and eager beneath her bra. Her core ached, heat coating her sex, leaving her panties damp. She could feel everything from the soft play of his breath as he leaned in, gripping her upper arms to bring her to her feet, through to the brush of fabric across her skin. She'd lost. She hadn't believed it would come to this, and the sane part of her mind screamed a no before it just...well, shrugged an acceptance, whispered a wicked *enjoy,* and ran off to find a comfy chair and a good book.

With the hold in place, he turned her around, cupping her chin once she proved she wasn't going to collapse, and lifted her gaze to meet his. *Strange, I should be fighting this. Screaming at him to let me go.* Yet she didn't want to, couldn't find the desire to fight.

"You can say no. I'd respect your choice." His eyes darkened with lust, but the words—he would back off if she demanded he do so. She didn't need to hear him say it to understand that Kyle understood how the game was played. This was what set him apart from those who would push and take what wasn't given. Despite everything, including the way his cock was trying tented his jeans, Kyle wouldn't step over that line.

"I made my choice before we walked into this room." She ran the tip of her tongue over her bottom lip. "This is what we both want. If—if I had won, you'd have followed through as well."

He smiled, a mischievous light dancing in his eyes. "Oh, I might have renegotiated the terms."

No *might* about it, but would she have let him?

"Last chance to back out."

"I don't need to." Carolyn tipped her chin. "I can take anything you dish out."

"Oh." He chuckled, the sound rich and delicious. "We'll see about that." He still held her chin in his right hand and ran his thumb over her jaw line. "If you need to stop, scream *red*."

Red. The same generic safe word she used with her clients, yet what they were about to do was far from generic. Would he understand why she wanted something else? *And why does it matter if he understands or not?* "Vegas."

His gaze narrowed, an understanding followed by a barely perceptible nod. "Vegas it is then."

She tried to slip her hands free from the belt. The struggle was done, she'd agreed to submit for the time being, so there was no need for the bonds. He slid his hand up from her chin to her hair, easing his fingers into the length and tightened, pulling her close. She gasped, forced onto her toes by his grip, her back arching as she tried to pull away. The backs of her legs touched the edge of the bed and between that, his grip, and the position he had taken in front of her, she had no way to escape—even if she hadn't agreed to submit.

"You won't try to escape unless I tell you to do so." He was close, his breath caressing her lips with each word. "Understood?"

"Yes…"

"Sir."

"Yes, Sir." Carolyn paled. Of course he'd want an honorific, but she'd never used one like this before. Calling someone Master because of their skills with leather or whips or ropes wasn't the same as calling someone Sir as a submissive. *Bottom, I'm bottoming, not submitting. It's not the same as submitting. He understands that, doesn't he?*

He tightened his grip in her hair, forcing a gasp of pain from her lips. Lips he claimed, tongue piercing between her lips, tasting her, taking her until her pulse raced and breath burned in her lungs. She arched, welcoming his kiss, dueling with him for control despite the way her hands remained bound. He growled, trapping her between the edge of the bed and his body, his grip merciless. Each thrust of his tongue demanded that she submit beneath the onslaught.

It should have frightened her, but she embraced his sensual attack.

He broke the kiss, pulled back from her lips, and used the grip in her hair to turn her. Without warning he forced her down, bent her over the edge of the bed, and slid his free hand down to her pants. Fingers fumbled for a moment before he found the button and zipper. Both parted under his touch as he grabbed the waistband and yanked, pulling them down to her knees. A moment later her panties followed.

She whimpered, tensing beneath his grasp. "What…"

"Before I enjoy the taste of this." He reached in, cupping her sex, parting her swollen nether lips with one finger. "We have a small matter to deal with." He entered her with a single finger, stroking her three times before he pulled out and set his hand on bared bottom. "Attacking me wasn't a wise idea."

Wise? It had been the only thing that had made sense at the time. "It wasn't, exactly, an attack." The protest sounded weak even to her ears. "I was fighting back against—"

His hand lifted only to land with a sharp crack against her left buttock before she had a chance to complete her thought. Carolyn gasped, lifted onto her toes by the blow. Pain and heat merged, rippling through her ass and into her sex.

"You fought back and then drew a knife on me." A second blow landed, then a third.

She hissed, wriggling in an attempt to get away, but he held her in place. "Stop it!"

Four, five, and six rang out in quick succession. "You're not in a position to give orders." Five more blows, alternating between left and right cheeks. "You know what to say if this is too much for you." Again and again he struck, adding heat and pain with each new smack.

Carolyn gasped, arching, fighting for a moment longer before she lifted her ass to meet each new blow. Her pussy clenched and tightened with the strikes. Heat grew, slick and needful, until it coated her inner walls, slipping down over her nether lips, and coated her clit. With her eyes closed, the needs to accept and complain combined until all she could do was whimper. She lost count of the strikes. The number no longer mattered, only the sensations that claimed her body, pushing her higher until a wall, one that she had denied, shattered.

Tears seeped down her cheeks, silent at first until the first full sob escaped.

A hand rubbed at her bottom, spreading the warmth. Strong fingers massaged, breaking any spots of tension, and still she cried.

"Let it go." His voice was firm, strong, offering a mental hand should she need it. "You've carried too much for too long. Let it go and let me take care of you, take control. You're safe with me, Carolyn. I promise that; you'll always be safe with me."

No, not always, but for now at least he was right.

She blinked, bringing the tears back under control. A weight lifted from her chest and she took a deep breath, clearing her mind. It still hurt, still burned, but the pleasure outweighed the pain. All through this, his hand continued to move across her buttocks, massaging, stroking until her body began to respond to his touch. Her hips lifted, buttocks pressing into his touch even as she shifted her thighs farther apart. Only the constraints of her clothing prevented her from spreading them farther.

He dipped his working hand between her thighs, cupping her sex. "You're sopping wet, my girl."

She groaned and pressed back into his hand. He'd delved into her body once before, only a finger, but it had been enough to tease her with the idea of more. And yes, she wanted more than a single finger. Needed to feel him, his cock, thick and heavy, pressed between her thighs. She turned her head, looking back over her

Take Down

shoulder. "Fuck me, please…"

He chuckled and withdrew his hand. "Not yet, sweetness." He shifted both hands to her hips, holding her in place before he used that grip to ease her onto the bed, rolling her onto her side so her back faced him, her hands still bound. "These need to go." He reached down, tugging at her pants and panties, yanking them free before he tossed them to the floor. "Better."

She wasn't about to disagree.

"I'm going to untie you for a moment, and you're not going to fight me, are you?"

"No, Sir."

Something caught her attention. The clink of chain as something was lifted and then placed on the bed near her head. The manacles? That would make sense. Kyle removed the belt from her wrists, and he urged her to place her hands by the top of the bed, close to the headboard. He slipped the chain through the rails that made up the headboard before he locked the manacles on her wrist. Only then did she realize it couldn't be the same set he'd used on her ankle.

Where had he pulled that one from?

It doesn't matter. Relax and enjoy.

"Roll onto your stomach."

Carolyn obeyed, her heart racing as she felt him move around the other side of the bed. Her bottom lip caught between her teeth as he took hold of her ankles. He spread them until she felt a pull, letting her know that she'd reached the edge of her comfort.

"Don't move unless I tell you to. If that means you need to beg, then you'll beg."

Her jaw tightened. She wasn't going to beg. Sure, she'd agreed to bottom to him, but lowering herself to that level of submission? No way in hell.

A loud slap caught her left buttock, and she hissed, arching under the blow.

"You can deny it, fight it, but it will happen, my girl. I'm going to push you until you let the final walls down."

"They're gone," she snapped at him.

"Like hell they are." A fresh smack caught her off guard. "If they were, you wouldn't fight the idea of begging." He rubbed his hand over the fresh sting. "By the time we're done, you'll be free of that baggage. Every single piece of it."

CAROLYN LAY BEFORE him, naked from the waist down, her thighs spread, hands bound above her head as she rested on her stomach. Kyle was left struggling with his teenage self who wanted nothing more than to scream in delight and pounce before she changed her mind. He swallowed hard, cursing his rigid cock as he brought his desires under control. You couldn't be a Dominant until you first learned to control yourself, yet he'd never before been presented with temptation like the woman before him.

Her backside glowed a deep red from the spanking, but as he watched, the color eased by fractions. The rich hue turned softer, taunting him to add to the color once more. He let his gaze move from her buttocks to the pink, fleshy lips between her thighs. Soft coral in places, edged with tempting red, glistening from a need that was undeniable. Only a small strip of curls had been left on her mound, and none edged the outer lips of her pussy, making it easy to go down on her.

He shuddered, reining in his control, except he wanted to taste her.

Not yet.

"You enjoyed the spanking." His words were little more than a growl.

She tensed but didn't speak.

"Lies, even by omission, won't make it any easier for you. Answer me, did you enjoy the spanking?" He knew the answer, but forcing her to respond was something he now needed.

She murmured something into the bedding.

"It's not an honest answer if I can't hear it, and I punish dishonesty." He bent down and picked up the belt he'd removed from her wrists. "Perhaps that's what you want."

"No." She shook her head and then turned to look at him. "Yes, okay, I enjoyed the spanking."

Would she enjoy the touch of the belt? He reached down and pushed up her shirt, uncurled the belt, and traced the tip off the leather down the length of her spine.

She moaned, arching under the caress of the leather.

"Good, because I enjoyed spanking you. I'd like to do more than spank, but I don't have my toys with me." He eased the belt away from her back and slapped the leather against the palm of his hand. "But I have this."

She flinched at the sound, her thighs clenched and parting a little more.

"Beg me not to use the belt." He smiled, wondering if she would do it or would call out her safe word.

Carolyn snarled and shook her head.

"Hmm." He snapped the belt against the bedding by her hip, knowing she would feel the rush of air. "One last chance, my girl." His girl. Was she his? No, he wasn't going to think about that. There was only this room, this time between them, and nothing else mattered. "Well then, let's see how you respond. "

Before she could react, Kyle brought the tip of the belt down on her still-pink ass, snapping it back so the blow was more sting than pain. This wasn't about punishment but pushing buttons, seeing how she took to being a submissive plaything for a Dominant.

Carolyn hissed, her buttocks tensing. "Bastard!"

"No, I can actually deny that allegation." He smirked and landed two more quick snaps, taking care not to repeat where the leather landed. "My parents were, and still are, happily married."

"Evil asshole!"

He laughed, striking four times. "Now that I can admit to." Each blow caused her to squirm. Her full ass tempted him as she hissed and whimpered. Color changed with the blows, the strikes white for a moment before turning to deep red and then fading as he continued to space the stinging slaps from his belt. God, how he wanted to take that ass, but it wasn't ready. She wasn't ready.

"Why don't you just fuck me and get it over with!" Carolyn howled as he finished a series of five rapid blows.

"Oh, is that what you think this is about? That I'm a wham, bam, and all over in a matter of minutes man?" He leaned down, resting the belt over her rosy-red backside. "You've got so much to learn, little mistress. By the time I'm done with you, I'll be branded into your body, your heart, and your soul. You won't ever be able to look at a man, think about sex again, without remembering the feel of my hands on your body." He knew, even as he gave life to the words, that he meant what he said.

Kyle shuddered. He was lost. When this was over, he'd never be able to look at another woman the same way again. Carolyn, this beautiful, confident woman, would remain with him. It didn't matter that he wanted to deny it, wanted to pretend he would be able to move on, but he couldn't embrace the lie.

I'm fucked.

Yes, he was, but he'd never admit it. Not to Carolyn, not to anyone but himself.

"You're insane!"

"Maybe, but I'm also honest." He reached between her thighs and slid two fingers into her hot, clenching sex.

"God!" She arched, hips rolling and bucking until she shuddered and lay still. "You could have warned me."

"Where would be the fun in that?" He pumped his fingers slowly in and out, watching her fight to maintain control. His cock throbbed, balls tight against the base of his erection. Damn, if he didn't claim her soon, he'd come in his jeans. "You're soaked, my girl. Hot, wet, and ready for me, aren't you?"

"Yes, so do it already!" She looked back over her shoulder, her lips swollen from their earlier kiss. "Fuck me."

"Are you begging?" He knew she wasn't.

"Like hell!"

Take Down

He smiled, picking up the pace, curving his fingers within her until he found that small indentation.

Carolyn's hips jerked. "No… You… Oh, God!"

Wet heat surged around his fingers as he continued to stroke and press against that sensitive spot. "You've got no choice, little mistress. Not in this. Not unless you use your safe word." The power was in her hands, and they both knew that. Just as he knew she wouldn't use it. Wouldn't push to end the scene. Her pride wouldn't let her, so he had to be the one to keep a close watch on her reactions.

He could feel everything she did. Each twitch, the way her breath hitched and shuddered through her body. Tiny ripples of tension as her muscles tightened and released, highlighted by small beads of sweat that glistened over her taut skin. Her arousal filled the air, a heady musk that begged and pleaded. Each soft sound focused his attention a little more until he understood what was happening.

Dom space—that moment when a Dom understood, knew without a doubt that they were in charge, running the scene. Nothing escaped his notice, and that Dominant part of his soul screamed in triumph.

"I have to… No, stop, I don't…yes…" Words spilled from her lips as she writhed under his touch. The tight clenching of her slick core now came in spasms, letting him know she was close.

"Let it happen." He growled the words as he leaned down, increasing the pace with his fingers. "You need to let go."

"N-no. I…w-won't."

Kyle smiled, delight claimed him, and he lifted his free hand, and brought it down with a sharp slap on her upturned ass.

Her pussy clenched, tight, hard, and rippling around his fingers even as she bucked, crying out when the orgasm claimed her. Slick desire soaked his hand, coating his fingers and palm as she moved, writhing on him, and still he pushed. Touching, stroking, moving his fingers in and out of her core as wave after wave forced its devastating path through her body.

Only when the shudders finally eased to a manageable level did Kyle ease his fingers free and bring them to his lips. "I wonder if you taste as good as you smell."

Carolyn turned her head, looking back over her shoulder at him, her eyes dazed, lips softly parted.

Kyle met her gaze, holding it as he licked and sucked his fingers clean, groaning in delight before he finally spoke again. "Beautiful, just like the woman it came from."

Take Down

Chapter Twelve

What has he done to me?

Carolyn shuddered, trying to force order into her thoughts. He'd taken her, marked her within and without, and still he hadn't fucked her. If he could reduce her to this without actual sex, what would happen when he fucked her for real? Her mind reeled. He'd done this with only his hand, a simple restraint, and a belt. No real toys.

Was that the mark of a true Dominant?

She shook her head, scrambling to find a way to speak, to tell him she'd had enough even as the Dominant side of her mind screamed its defiance, but that wasn't the part that worried her. No, a new voice, a quiet, frightened voice had spoken for the first time. A sensual, submissive side that wanted more, needed more, and would do anything it could to prevent Carolyn from ending this.

His strong hands stroked her sides, down over her hips, and back up again, soothing her still-quivering flesh until she was finally able to catch her breath. He didn't speak and she didn't resist, not even when he silently urged her onto her back and pushed up her shirt and bra, baring her breasts. Her nipples throbbed, and even the light, almost casual touch of his fingers as he'd revealed them caused her to arch and gasp. They were hard, aching, and connected through an intricate set of nerve endings that led directly to her clit.

A zipper parted, jeans hitting the floor at the side of his bed, and something in a silver package was set half under the pillow beneath her head.

Condom?

That made sense. It wasn't as though either of them had paperwork with them.

The bed shifted with the introduction of his weight, focusing her attention back on the man.

"With me again?"

She blinked, swallowed hard, and met his gaze. "Y-yes...Sir." It wasn't as hard to add on the Sir this time as it had been before. Her Dominant side protested, but instead of a scream, it was more of a grumble.

"Good." He knelt on the bed between her ankles, shifting his weight until his hands found her still-parted thighs. "Look at me."

Carolyn obeyed, her stomach knotting, twisting as she watched him. Her sex pulsed with the rapid beat of her heart as she let her gaze drift down for a moment to his thick cock before she lifted her eyes back up to meet his. She'd known from their fight, from the feel of his body against hers, that he would be satisfactory, but this?

"Like what you see?" He smiled as he moved over her, resting his hands on either side of her head, his hips between her thighs.

"Yes, Sir." God, did she. Her cunt clenched, hips lifting in a silent plea.

"Good." The head of his cock brushed against her swollen nether lips. "But not yet." He shifted, lowering his mouth toward her breasts.

No, she didn't want to be teased anymore. She wanted his cock buried deep within her body. Needed the feel of it stretching her inner walls, pushing at her until she screamed in release over and over again.

The tip of his tongue flickered over her left nipple. Carolyn groaned, tipping her head back as her hips lifted, her clit aching in time to the touches to her nipple. Kyle's fingers found and closed around her right nipple, pinching and rolling it, matching the movements on her left nipple with his tongue, teeth, and lips. Small pinches with teeth and fingers, flicks, nips, and pressure all tormented her tender nipples. She bucked, trying to find a way to push his cock into her body, but somehow she managed to keep her thighs parted.

Each time her hips moved beneath him, his cock tormented her swollen sex by brushing and almost but never quite parting her lips. He laughed, the sound vibrating through her trapped nipple even as he shifted his hips, moving his cock so it stroked back and forth

Take Down

over her clit.

Every nerve ending in her body reacted, stripped of any protective coverings, leaving her a raw, needful bundle of nerves. She couldn't take much more of this, didn't have the strength to protest, but neither did she have the ability to beg for his cock.

I have to. If I want this, I have to beg.

The Dominant side whimpered in protest, but the voice was weaker now, lacking conviction.

"You're close, little one. I can see it, taste it in the air." He lifted his head away from her breast and smiled down at her. No arrogance in his smile or in his voice, just knowledge. "But the wall is still there. We both know it."

Wall, yes, she knew there was a wall. She could feel it.

"Let it fall."

No.

She needed that wall. It if fell, how would she build it back up again? How could she protect herself?

"I won't hurt you."

Yes, he would. They would part ways once this job was over and done with. He would take her back to Minnesota, and then she'd never see him again. That hurt. The very idea of it hurt more than she wanted to admit, but the knowledge was there nevertheless. She whimpered, shaking her head. This wasn't what she had signed up for. He had to know that, understand that, so why was he pushing?

"You can do this. There's nothing to be afraid of."

What did he know about it? He was a man. A Dominant and... she was a Dominant. Except with him.

He lowered his lips to her neck, nibbling, licking, and teasing a path over her sweat-soaked skin. Her hands clenched, eyes closed as she fought against the shivers. Her skin tightened, nerves raw as she moved beneath him. Each new touch of his lips was matched by a stroke of his cock over her clit, sending her higher, closer to the edge of breaking, but still she fought to maintain her sanity.

"Please," she whispered, barely aware that she'd spoken.

"You know what to say." One finger flicked over her right nipple. "You know what I need to hear." Another flick of finger matched by a stroke of cock and nip of teeth. "It's in your hands."

Her hands. His. It didn't matter. Her body threatened a revolt if her mind didn't submit. "I can't. You know I can't." She could. He knew it. She knew it.

"Lie."

Yes, it was. She closed her mouth, fighting to keep the words trapped within. Her body fought back, lifting and rolling her hips, brushing against his thick cock, adding to the pressure within her core. She'd had one orgasm. Her body shouldn't be this greedy for a second, third, or however many more he offered her. The band of muscles that stretched across her body from hip to hip rippled in need, the hunger building within her body until she was certain he would push her over the edge. Her hands clenched, nails digging into her palms. She wouldn't cry out, wouldn't let him know what was happening. This orgasm would be for her, and her alone, and there was nothing he could do about it.

He stopped his cock so close to her clit that she could feel its presence, but it no longer touched her. No movement to bring her over the brink. His finger no longer touched her nipple, and only his breath now caressed her throat.

"No…" she whimpered, arching to try to touch him.

"Do not move." He growled.

She flattened against the bed with a ragged sob, opening her eyes to look up at him. "Please, don't stop."

He didn't speak.

"Kyle, don't do this to me." Her core wept, her inner thighs slick with need and frustration.

Nothing. He held there, watching her, their gazes locked.

"Fuck me, please," she pleaded. Once the words began, she couldn't stop them. "Fuck me, I'm begging you. Kyle, Sir, please, I need your cock. I need to feel it in me. Owning me. Claiming me."

Take Down

He smiled and reached for the wrapped condom, easing back onto his knees. "Thank you." His voice was soft. The wrapper tore in his grip, and he rolled the condom down over his thick, erect cock, smoothing it into place. "Thank you for trusting me."

"Please, just do it. Don't make me wait any longer, Sir," Carolyn pleaded, lifting her hips to him as he settled back down, pressing the head of his cock at her entrance. "Yes, do it. God, fuck me!" A demand and a plea all rolled into one.

Kyle thrust into her, piercing her to the core. His thick cock stretched her walls, filling her as she gasped, lifted her legs, and locked her heels behind his backside. Yes, he'd told her not to move, but she wasn't in control of her actions now. Her body ruled her mind, not the other way around, but he didn't complain, didn't correct her. Instead he used her new position to enter her farther, filling her to the brink.

"Yes!" she hissed, lifting and rolling her hips, moving on his cock.

"Easy." He slapped her left buttock, the blow light but stinging. "I set the pace, not you."

She yelped. Not fair. She wanted to move, needed to react. She couldn't hold on much longer. Her body threatened to shatter around his erection as he began to shift his weight, teasing her with slow, deep, firm strokes that set her body alight and added more fuel to the fire with each new thrust.

"Soon, sweet one. Very soon." The words were forced, his face as mask of concentration.

Her inner walls tightened and rippled, closing and releasing on his cock, setting the pace until he groaned and gave in. His thrusts became stronger, rocking her, rocking the bed as they moved together. Beads of sweat formed and rolled into her eyes. Her hands fisted and released in time to his thrusts, and she cried out.

"So close, so damn close!" Why couldn't she come? Why did that orgasm linger on the edge, unable to take the final leap? She'd surrendered, given him everything he wanted.

But not everything I need.

"Beg for it," he growled, his fingers gripping her hips, holding her off the bed as he filled her over and over again, his balls slapping against her sex. Slick, needful sounds spilled into the air, combining with the creak of the bed and their labored breathing.

"Let me come, sir. Please, I need to come!" She didn't even think about it.

His grip tightened on her hips, small points of pain that she knew would leave bruises. Knew but didn't care. "Come for me," Kyle commanded.

It hit, ripping through Carolyn's body without mercy. Heat, need, muscles tightening, clenching even as her mind lost ability to track thought. Sensation ruled as she bucked, lifting on him, slamming back down on his cock, inner walls closing around his cock. A small part of her was aware of his own release, the sound of his roar, the feel of his cock swelling, filling her that little more, and still they moved together.

Moments passed, minutes, she didn't know, didn't care. Their shared release took control of the time and dumped them back down on the bed when it was done. A mingling of sweat-soaked limbs, aching muscles, and gulped breaths.

Kyle moved first, reaching up for the manacles that restrained her wrists, releasing her before he rolled onto his side and gathered her to his chest. In silence he wrapped her close, nuzzling her neck, his lips finding her pulse where he then placed a soft, tender kiss.

He didn't say anything, and she didn't need him to speak, not now. There would be time, perhaps, for talking later, but now all she wanted to do was fall asleep in his arms.

Take Down

Chapter Thirteen

Kyle looked back into the bedroom where Carolyn had slept. Had it really only been a couple of hours ago that they'd enjoyed each other's bodies? He shook his head and glanced down the hall toward the bathroom. Right now, she was showering, cleaning herself off, removing any and all traces of their shared passion before their transport arrived. He couldn't blame her. He'd done the same thing—well, mostly. A quick rinse, clean shirt and boxers, but he could still smell her.

How was that possible?

Perhaps he could still smell them because he'd looked at the bedroom?

No, he'd stripped the bed, bundling the bedding up and placing it in a bag near the door. The boss would send someone in to clean the ranch house after the job was done. That was standard operating practice.

Yet he could still smell her, taste her— Shit, he could still feel her moving on his cock.

Stop it.

The door to the bathroom opened, and she stepped out, her long purple hair pulled back into a thick braid. Pity, he liked it loose. Not his call. None of this was his call. The job was almost done. He'd deliver her, finish the contract, and report for duty. Maybe there'd be another job already lined up for him? Something that would take his mind off the woman who had rocked his world and somehow seared a way into his heart.

It was just sex.

Yeah, right. Even he didn't believe that.

"Everything okay?" she asked, her voice softer than it had been the night before.

"Yeah, they'll be landing in ten minutes."

Her eyes widened and she shook her head. "So soon, I thought... Never mind. Doesn't matter." The mask slammed back into place.

Gone was the softer, beautiful, sensual woman she had been a few hours ago. The Mistress was back. She lifted her chin, pushed back her shoulders, and met his gaze. "Do we walk out to meet them?"

"When the plane lands, yes."

"Understood." Something flashed across her eyes. "My sister will be waiting."

* * * *

The plane, a Cessna Citation CJ3 that had already made a stop prior to landing here in order to top up on fuel, was comfortable enough. The fact that there'd been a stop meant that there'd be no need to fuel before landing in Minnesota, reducing the chances of Carolyn's escape. No, the men on the plane hadn't told her the escape part, but it made sense. Not that it mattered. She had neither the desire nor the energy to try. At this point she wanted to see Cassandra, look her in the eyes, and ask her what the hell she was playing at.

There would be tears, screaming, shouting, and then it would be over. Whatever paperwork Cassandra needed her to sign would be seen to and then...then what?

Return to Vegas?

What about her car? Had it been discovered? Was anyone looking for her?

Too many questions.

With a sigh she leaned back in the chair, tempted to close her eyes and shut out the world, but her gaze kept moving to the seat where he sat. The man who had turned her world upside down and, now once this was done with, would walk away without so much as a backward glance. She couldn't blame him, wouldn't blame him— except she did.

Kyle.

He had stripped away her walls, and she'd let him. Worked with him to bring them down, and now she would be left to build them back up on her own.

Well, she'd done it before, and she would do it again. She didn't

Take Down

need him—but damn, she wanted him.

"We'll be landing in less than an hour," a male voice, one that didn't belong to Kyle, announced as he walked back in from the cockpit.

"Thanks, Michael." Kyle looked up.

Michael, not Mike, that had been the way the blond-haired, blue-eyed man with a soft easy-going Midwestern tones had introduced himself. His speech in complete contrast to the formality he insisted on with his name.

"You need anything, Miss Grant?" Michael made his way to her chair.

"No, I'm good." She met his gaze, drawn into the depths of his blue eyes for a second before she forced herself to take a breath. Damn Kyle. Even his friends were good looking. Except Michael wasn't, not exactly. A small scar at the corner of his left eye and another under his chin didn't detract from his appearance. No, it was something in his eyes. Not the color but a look that told her stay away, stand back, don't touch, run, don't walk away from this man.

"No problem, just making sure." His smile never touched his eyes, leaving them...empty? No, that wasn't the word.

It doesn't matter, I'm never going to have to see or deal with him again. Michael, no last name offered, turned and walked back to Kyle before he dropped into the empty seat nearest to his colleague.

"Anything interesting happen?" Kyle looked up.

Carolyn tried to look away, but her gaze returned to Kyle time and again. Each time she looked at him, she chided herself. She didn't need the memories; she'd forget him within a couple of months. Well, maybe not forget, but at least it wouldn't hurt when she thought about him, about what they'd shared and...shit, she was doing it again.

"Nothing much, a couple of new jobs on the books, but they're already being parceled out. I've pulled one that I start in a week." Michael glanced back at Carolyn who quickly looked away. "I'll fill you in after we land."

When she couldn't hear what was being said.

Her jaw clenched. Did they really think she'd say anything? If there was a risk that she'd press charges—could she do that?

Yes, but why would I want to?

Her gaze flickered back to Kyle. She could do it, turn them in, press charges for kidnapping her, but she'd only hurt herself in this. He'd been hired to do a job, and the contract would trace back to her sister. He'd be punished for a decision Cassandra had made, and was that fair?

He could have turned down the job.

Yes, he could, and then someone else, someone who didn't care if she was hurt, humiliated, or worse might have taken on the task.

And I'd have never met Kyle. Never known his touch, his kiss, his... She looked away and closed her eyes, knowing if she didn't that the tears blurring her vision would spill and the last of her secrets would then be bared to him.

* * * *

They hadn't spoken since leaving the plane, not even during the drive through the small, sleepy Minnesota town. Michael had remained with the plane, overseeing a few things before he would then report back in, but that hadn't mattered. It didn't take two of them to escort Carolyn to her sister.

And then what?

They'd part company. There was nothing else to it. Kyle had known that what they had shared would end like this from the moment Kyle had admitted his attraction Carolyn. It should never have gone as far as it did. Shit, he'd known how wrong it was, but it hadn't stopped him. In truth, he hadn't tried that hard to talk himself out of it.

He glanced over at her and turned his attention back to the road. *Drive. Keep an eye on the road.* He knew that was what he should do, but the temptation to look at her, to take in the curve of her lips, the arrogant, obviously forced, tilt to her chin, the set of her jaw, and the way her hands clenched and unclenched on her lap was too great a temptation. She didn't want this meeting, didn't want to see her sister, and a part of him, a huge part, wanted to pull off to the side of the road and say to hell with the contract.

"We don't have to do this." Kyle spoke before his common sense had a chance to kick in. *Shit, what am I saying? This is a job, one I signed up for, and I can't back down now, not when it's almost over and done with.*

"Yes, we do."

"No, I mean we can turn around, find a place to talk. If you…"

"You're the hired hand, remember? That's what you told me, so you get the job done and pick up your paycheck. Then you never have to see me again." She didn't look at him.

Hired hand. Yes, that was what he'd used to describe himself, but never in a million years had he thought hearing it from her lips would hurt. "All right, then let's get this over and done with."

"Indeed."

His jaw clenched, but he didn't respond. There was no point. They'd both made their mistakes and they'd live with it.

Five minutes later he turned off the engine and stepped out of the car, intending to open her door, but she beat him to it. She didn't look at him, didn't even acknowledge his presence, but walked straight to the main door, opened it, and walked in without waiting to knock or see if anyone would let her in.

Of course. This was her home. She'd know her way around.

"Ms. Grant, she's expecting you." A woman rose from behind a heavy dark wood desk near the entrance. Yes, the house was a home, but it was also a place of business. Had it been that way when Carolyn had lived here?

"Yes, of course she is." Emotionless, that was the only way to describe Carolyn's answer. "She's in the office?"

"Yes."

"Thought so." Carolyn glanced back at him, and for a moment he saw something. Pain. Sorrow. He didn't know for certain, but it flashed across her eyes and was gone. The mask of professional calm slammed back down into place, locking everything else behind a door that only she held the key to.

"Mr. Orion, if you'd wait here please. I know Ms. Grant will want to speak with you after this matter is taken care of." The secretary smiled and gestured to a handful of chairs. "I'm sure she'll be with you soon."

"No, I don't think so." He ignored the chairs and followed Carolyn.

"Mr. Orion, please…"

"CAROLYN, OH GOD, you don't know how good it is to see you again." Cassandra pushed back her chair and hurried around and Carolyn into a hug before she had a chance to protest.

She tensed, uncertain what to do. Of all the things she thought might happen, this hadn't been one of them. She lifted her arms and tried to return the embrace but knew it came off as stiff. "Cassandra, I'm—"

"He's dead, but you know that, don't you?" Her sister broke the embrace and stepped back. "Yes, of course you know. Sorry." Cassandra swallowed and shook her head. "You should have called me. We could have flown you home and then— But no, you had to be stubborn."

"This isn't my home." Until that moment, until the words found a life of their own, Carolyn hadn't accepted that fact. But here, now, with her twin, she knew it to be true.

"Of course it is. Don't talk like that. Even with the bitch queen around, this will always be your home. That's why I need you here. She's going to get everything unless you sign off on Father's papers." Cassandra turned, moving back to the desk where she grabbed a navy blue folder. "You can read it for yourself, but it's a mess. He wrapped everything up in her name unless we both sign off in front of his lawyer."

Carolyn looked at the folder. "This is all about this damned house and the business? You yanked me here, had me kidnapped, because you couldn't be bothered to come down to Vegas yourself, with the blasted lawyer and—"

"Of course I couldn't leave things. If I turn my back for a moment, she's digging into things. You don't know what it's been like since you ran away." Cassandra scowled and dropped the folder back on the desk. "But you're back now. We can get this sorted and then settle you in. She'll hate that; you know she will. By the time she gets back from her shopping trip in the cities, it will all be taken care of, and there'll be nothing she can do about it."

The door opened behind her and closed again, but she didn't turn to see who had entered. No doubt it was either the lawyer or Cassandra's secretary.

Or Kyle.

She wanted to turn, to see for herself who it was who had entered the room, but turning her back on Cassandra was a mistake she had no intention of making.

"Cassandra…Cassie…listen to me, listen to yourself." Carolyn sighed and walked over to the desk. "You've no idea what could have happened when you— The man who—"

"Did he hurt you? If he has…" Cassandra's eyes narrowed, her voice growing harsh. "Bruises! You bastard, what did you do to her? And don't deny it!" Her gaze shifted back to Carolyn, the words confirming that the noise earlier had been Kyle entering the room. "Tell me, and I'll have him charged with-with…"

"With kidnapping? Well, that would be interesting, especially as I'd have to testify that you were behind the kidnapping." Carolyn arched an eyebrow at her twin. "You damned silly fool, you didn't think this through. You sent a stranger after me. I could have been hurt, ended up in hospital, or even killed."

"No, she didn't think it through, but she wouldn't be the first client to then try to place the blame elsewhere. It's why Brent makes sure that all the paperwork is in order." Kyle's strong voice rang out through the office even as he walked across the room. "If you took a moment to think, you'd remember that, Ms. Grant."

Cassandra took a step back, paling before she lifted her chin. "Of course I remember that. I'm not a fool. I was merely taken aback by all of this." A coldness claimed her words. "Did you harm her?"

"No."

"No." Carolyn tried not to react to his words. He hadn't harmed her, not in the traditional sense of the word. "Of course he didn't."

"Then why bring it up?" Cassandra turned her ice-blue eyes back on her twin.

"Because it was proof that you didn't think this through." She sighed and rubbed the back of her neck. "Fine, I'll look at the papers. We'll get them signed and that will be the end of it. I'll return to my life in Vegas and—"

"Return to Vegas? Why would you do that? You belong here, with me. We both know that," Cassandra protested. "Look, you're tired. Go to your room, get a shower, change into something more suitable. Your old clothes are still in your closet. They'd be more suitable than what you're wearing right now." Her sister paused for a breath but then continued on. "It will all work out in the end. You know that. We both know that."

"If everything else has been taken care of, I'll need the final paperwork from our end of the contract, and then I'll be out of your hair." Kyle turned to look at Carolyn, his voice and eyes softening for a moment. "Unless you need something from me, Lyn?" He held out a hand, offering it.

Without thinking she took it, barely aware of the card he pressed into her grasp. "No, I don't think... I'll be fine." *No, I won't be. Not without you. Damn you, don't leave me here. You can't just leave me here.*

She ached. Every part of her soul demanded that she move into his arms. God, this wasn't fair. She wanted to feel him wrap around her for a moment, an hour, a lifetime, but that was foolish. Of course it was. He was nothing but the man who'd been hired to bring her home, and she would always be nothing more to him than an assignment.

Take Down

"Then I'll get out of here." Kyle nodded at Cassandra who opened a file, signed the bottom of one page, and handed it off to him. "Ladies, it's been a pleasure." He caught Carolyn's gaze on that last word.

She shivered, a deep ache of need and fear claiming her, but she didn't move. It was over between them; in fact, it had never begun. She'd never see him again, and it was time to accept that and move on.

Chapter Fourteen

"Snap out of it, man. You've been moping around this place for five days now." Michael slapped him on the back, half knocking him out of the chair. "Come on, there's a new server at the diner, pretty little thing. You look like you could do with a good meal, and a shower. So I suggest you get out of here before you grow roots in that chair."

Kyle growled and sat up, glaring at the man. "Since when were you interested in what I did or didn't do with my life?"

"Since you decided to inflict your mood on the rest of us." Michael sat on the edge of his desk and folded his arms. "What the hell crawled up your ass?"

"Nothing," Kyle snapped.

"Bullshit." Michael snorted.

"I have to agree with Michael," Harvey Brent announced as he walked into the main room from his office at the back. "You've spent the last couple of days either moping or growling. Spit it out. What's going on with you?"

Kyle turned and glared at the older man. In his early sixties, Brent walked with the posture of a military man unwilling to back down no matter what odds he faced. "It's not going to affect my work, so why is it any of your concern?" Kyle regretted the words the moment they gained life. "Look, I'm sorry, boss. It's just— Fuck, I don't know."

"Yes, you do, and if I'm any judge of the boys who work for me, it's about a girl." Brent pulled out a chair and sat down. "One you met on this last job. So, odds are it's one of the twins."

Michael let out a low whistle. "You fucked her, didn't you?"

Kyle looked away. "Don't know what you're talking about."

"Fuck, boy, you went there, didn't you?" Brent sighed and leaned his elbows on his thighs. "Of all the damned mistakes to make, you went and slept with a target."

"Could have been worse. He might have slept with a client."

Take Down

Michael grinned.

"Don't tempt fate." Brent rubbed his temples.

"Brent, there's not one man, or woman, working for you who'd do something that stupid." Michael paused and shifted his weight. "All right, I'd have said the same thing about sleeping with a target before today, but still—a client? Bad business practice."

Business. Right this was all about business. Kyle rolled out his shoulders and moved to his feet. "If you need to let me go over this mess, I'll understand." He'd hate it, but he'd accept it. What other choice did he have? He'd acted like a fool, stepped well over the line, and fucked the woman. *No, it was more than that.* He'd felt the walls shatter. That didn't happen unless there was something more between them.

So why hadn't she called him?

He'd put the card in her hand. She had his damned number. If there'd been something more between them than sex, she'd have reached out, right?

Unless... Fuck, did she think that was an offer of another booty call?

"I should kick your ass out of the door, you know that." Brent rubbed the back of his neck. "I thought you boys knew better than that. Target, client, doesn't matter. They're both off limits. It's one of the rules of the business."

"I'll pack up my shit and be out before the end of the day." Kyle would lose his friends and his job in the same blow, but he deserved this. He'd been an idiot, and there was no escaping that fact. He stood up and turned his attention to his desk. How long would it take to pack that up? Not long. For all of the time he spent in the office, he'd brought very little in the way of personal items into his workspace.

"Sit your damned ass down, Kyle." Brent snapped the order.

Kyle sat down. Hard.

"I said I should kick your ass out of the door, not that I would do it. Fuck, boy, you're not the first to make an idiot mistake, and you won't be the last."

Kyle wanted to believe that. "Yeah, I guess."

"Did you force her?"

"Hell no." He snapped his head up, meeting Brent's gaze. "I don't play that way."

"Needed to make sure. You boys play hard and a little kinky, if the rumors are to be believed," Brent continued, his voice calm.

"Yeah, but kinky and rape aren't the same thing, boss," Michael explained.

"True enough. Just covering bases here."

"Understood." It still irked Kyle. "Rape isn't my thing, isn't with most...erm, Dominants. Not unless the sub wants it as a game. Even then it's...well, talked through." He looked away, heat touching his cheeks. No way in hell was he explaining takedown scenes or other forms of edge play with his boss. Talk about taking TMI to extremes.

"Then I don't understand what the problem is. This was obviously more than a quick roll in the hay moment, or you wouldn't be pouting like this. So why haven't you called the woman?"

"Maybe he has, boss, and she's told him where to stick it."

"I haven't called," Kyle admitted and looked back at his desk.

"Why not?" Brent inquired.

"Because... Well, shit..." Why hadn't he called? He had the sister's number, the business line and... "I don't have her personal number, but I-I gave her my card. I'm not going to call her sister or the office to talk to her. Don't know who else will be listening in."

"With the office number?"

"Yeah... fuck." Kyle had put her in the same position. Why the hell hadn't he scribbled his cell number on the card? He rubbed his arm, feeling the bruise that had formed around the shallow cut Carolyn had given him.

"Well then, I'd say it was time to either man up and call the woman, or walk away and accept that the door has now closed, never to be opened again."

* * * *

Take Down

Carolyn Grant stepped out of the car, locking it behind her with a quick click of the button on her key fob before she turned her attention to the low office building on the edge of the industrial park. "I shouldn't be here," she murmured.

Maybe not, but Kyle hadn't reached out to her, so she had a choice. Move on or track him down. The fact that he'd given her his card had offered a shred of hope, though the small, annoying voice in the back of her mind had done its best to try to convince her he'd left the card in case she wanted another turn in the sack. She straightened her shoulders, lifted her chin, and took a step toward the building. If that was the case, she'd turn around and walk away.

Wouldn't she?

Maybe.

If one more night, afternoon, or hour with him was all she would be offered, she'd take it.

Masochist.

Dominant, not submissive. Except with him. Right, fine, she'd submitted in the bedroom that once, but that didn't make her submissive in general. She'd proved that to her sister when the documents had been presented and Carolyn had walked out. Instead of staying with her sister, Carolyn had walked out of the office after signing the ones that allowed Cassandra to keep the business from their stepmother's hands, but not the ones that would have shared responsibility of the company between the sisters.

Cassandra hadn't been pleased.

Carolyn's phone rang for the seventh time since she'd driven away from lawyer's office. She tugged it out of her pocket, checked the screen, and sighed. Cassandra. Just as it had been the previous six calls. Carolyn glanced at the main entrance to the office building, rolled her eyes, and hit the Accept button.

"Where the hell are you?" Cassandra yelled.

"Is there something you need?" Carolyn forced herself to remain calm.

"You walked out! How could you walk out like that? Don't you know what you've done?"

"Yes, I know. I've given you free rein with the business, the house, everything." Anyone else would be pleased about the situation, but not her twin.

"You were supposed to come home, sign all the papers, and then run this thing with me."

"Why?" Carolyn turned away from the office.

"B-because that's how it's supposed to be. We're twins. We work together."

Sisters bound not just by blood but the womb they had shared for nine months. "We'll always be twins, Cassie, and I'll always love you."

"So get your ass back here and sign the rest of these papers."

"No." Carolyn took a step away from the car.

"What?"

"I said no. I told you no in the office, and I'm repeating it now. I've no interest in signing those papers. No desire to run the company. I'll accept my smaller share of the estate and go back to my life."

"What life? You were working as a high-end call girl!"

Her fingers tightened around the phone. "Is that what you think I was doing?"

"It's what the report said. You were working as a—" There was a rustle of papers. "Professional femme Domme."

"Which is not the same thing as a call girl." Carolyn had to stay calm. Losing her temper and screaming down the phone at her sister wasn't the way to handle this.

"You were paid to have sex with people—men and women."

"No." Who the hell had told her that? "I never had sex with a paying client. That's not what my work was about." Was? Would she go back to it? And if she did, would it be in Vegas? It wasn't as though she could see herself setting up shop in Minnesota. Though there were some well-established groups in the state. Ones that had been running for years, with good rules and—*Oh hell no. I'm not about to talk myself into moving back here.*

Take Down

"Look, I don't care what it was about. I'm sorry I accused you of being a prostitute, but you can't tell me that your life in Vegas was so wonderful that you wouldn't drop it if something better came along."

No, Carolyn couldn't say that. "What I choose to do with my life is just that, my choice. Dad tried to back me into a corner, tried to get me to be his clone, and now you want me to do the same thing. I didn't do it for him. I won't do it for you."

"It's not like that. I-I need you."

"No, you don't. You've run the company without me for years. Even when Dad was still alive, you were the driving force for at least the last two years." Carolyn took a deep breath. "You don't need me; you want me. There's a difference. Don't make me hide from you the way I had to hide from Dad, okay?"

A low sob echoed through the phone. "Please…"

A band tightened around Carolyn's heart. This was her sister, her twin, and the last thing she wanted to do was hurt Cassandra. "I'll always be there for you, on the end of the phone, an e-mail, even visits, but I'm happy, Cassie. Really happy away from that mess, and I'm asking you to be happy for me."

For a moment there was nothing but silence, followed by a hiccupped sob. "I'll try…"

"That's all I ask of you."

* * * *

He had to call her, but not here, not where Michael and Brent might hear him. It didn't matter if she hung up or rejected the call—Well, yes it did matter, and he'd try again until he talked to her, but the point was he had to try. He sighed, pulled his phone and a piece of paper out of his jeans, and then walked around from the back door of the low office building the company owned. Orange and red-colored leaves rustled in the breeze, maple trees announcing the change of the seasons. Soon enough he'd be preparing for winter and the potential of subzero temperatures, ten feet of snow, and teasing Brent about his love of ice fishing.

A soft, familiar voice caught Kyle's attention as he walked to the front of the building, and he stopped, his gaze fixed on the delicious curves he'd grown to know well. Faded blue jeans caressed her legs, covering her hips and ass in a temptation of denim. Her long purple-dyed hair had been caught up in a pair of twin braids that his hands now itched to take hold of and use to control her in a kiss he prayed would steal her heart and mind, but he forced himself to remain still.

"That's all I ask of you."

He swallowed. Hard. Who was she talking to? A lover? Had there been one he hadn't known about? His research hadn't revealed one, and she sure as hell hadn't mentioned one.

"I'll stay for a couple of days, not at the house. We need space to work this out, Cassie."

Relief washed over him. The sister. Fine, he could cope with that.

"I'll talk with you tomorrow. Right now— Yes, I'll find a good hotel. No, I won't tell you where. Please don't ask me." She shifted her weight, turning toward the building.

He tensed, took a deep breath, and strode toward her.

Her eyes widened. "I've got to go. I'll call tomorrow." She paused only long enough to hear a reply and closed the phone, slipping it into the pocket of her jeans.

"I was about to call you." He held out his phone, along with the scrap of paper he'd used to write the number down on.

A slight smile touched her lips. "I guess you were."

"You're here to talk to Brent? Harvey Brent, the boss?" That was the only reason she'd be here, right? God, Kyle didn't want to hope that she'd come here for him. Not when the odds were against it.

"No." She ran a nervous tongue over her bottom lip. "I'm—shit. We need to..." She glanced away; color flushed her cheeks. "What we did, what we shared..."

"It shouldn't have happened." Better to admit that and get it out of the way.

Take Down

"No, but it did." She lifted her chin.

"I want it to happen again."

Her jaw tightened. "I'm not a—"

"No, not like that. Fuck." He growled and closed the gap between them. One hand slid into her hair, gathering her braids in a firm grip. "I want you. Need you. Not as a quick fuck. Not as a booty call. Not on a casual basis. I want you. All of you." He held her close, their lips a breath apart. "Say you want the same thing, or tell me to walk away. I can't do—"

"Yes."

"What?" His heart skipped a beat. "I…"

"I want you. All of you." She reached up, wrapping her arms around him. "I don't know where or what this will mean. I don't know if that means staying here or you moving with me or us both moving. Shit, I don't know if this will be a week, a month, or a year. All I know is—is if I don't try, if I don't follow my heart this once, then I'll regret it for the rest of my life." She leaned in, touching her lips to his before continuing. "And I'm done with regrets, with doubts, with waiting for a better moment. I want— No, I need you."

He claimed her lips, parting them with his tongue. The future, yes that was uncertain, but they'd figure it out one step at a time, and they'd do it together.